THE OFFROM

NIKKI ASHTON

The Offrom
Copyright © Nikki Ashton 2023

Published by Hudson Indie Ink
www.hudsonindieink.com

The Offrom/Nikki Ashton

An **office romance**.

*New Guy: Man, that girl at **reception** is hot.*

***Seasoned** Worker: Don't touch her, she and the boss have had an offrom for **like forever**.*

by YukonWillie April 2, 2009

CHAPTER ONE

"Natty, we've overslept. Get up, now!"

I rolled over in bed and groaned. My head was pounding, my throat was dry, and my arse felt like it had been kicked by a stallion. Another night spent helping my flatmate, Andrew, to get over a shit week at work.

"Just five more minutes," I said against my pillow.

"You have to get up now, Natalie!" Andrew yelled from the bathroom. "Have you forgotten that report Freddie needs today? I mean, I don't know how you can have forgotten," he continued, muttering loud enough for me to hear. "You went on about it for long enough last night. Telling me how you still had so much to do."

That had me sitting bolt upright. "Fuck." I threw the duvet back and scrambled out of bed. "Andrew, get out of the flipping shower now." I stumbled, almost falling head first into my wardrobe and stubbed my toe. "Fucker." Pushing clothes to one side I finally found what I was looking for. When I pulled out the black and white spotted dress I gave it a quick once over. "Shit." There was a jam stain on the front. I'd have to wear a brooch or something.

By the time I'd found the red shoes that I wanted to wear with it, I could hear Andrew singing, badly, in the shower. Rushing towards the horrendous noise, I mentally worked out how late I was going to be.

"Shift over and seriously, please don't use my scrubber to wash your balls with?" Pointing in the general direction of his ball sack, I looked him up and down.

"This one is mine," he protested as he moved further along the double shower to make room for me.

"No, it isn't. The white one is mine, the pink one is yours." Stepping inside, I grabbed the shower scrubber from him and studied it. "Remember the rhyme? Pink because your balls stink. White to make your tits bright." The dubious hairs entwined in the mesh made me shove it back at him. "I'll get myself a new one."

I squeezed shower gel onto my hand, built up a froth and attempted a quick wash. It wasn't ideal but I could no longer use something that had been around Andrew's ball sack.

"You've got half an hour to get to work," Andrew informed me.

"I know. I know." The soap suds rinsed off easily under the stream of water and I put my hand out for my shampoo but then changed my mind. My brain was already practically falling out in some kind of alcohol protest. Scrubbing my scalp wouldn't help matters. "What the hell were we drinking last night?" I called over my shoulder as we stood back-to-back under the shower.

"Shots, JD, rum, shots, vodka, *shots*."

He nudged me in the back with an elbow, so I dug one back.

"And *why* does my arse hurt?"

"The slide at the kid's park." He was out of the shower now, and I knew what was coming. "Can I—?"

"No. You'll have to wait until I finish."

"It's just a shit, Natty. What's wrong with that? You've seen my winky."

3

I rolled my eyes. "Please don't call it a winky. You're a twenty-nine year old man."

"But can I go for a poo or not?"

"Not!"

After the quickest shower ever and racing around like someone doing Supermarket Sweep, I was moving out of the door yelling goodbye to Andrew.

Thankfully, my office was only a ten-minute bus ride away and the bus stop was outside our flat, *and* a bus turned up just as I walked through the front door of our building. Someone was certainly looking down on me because at only six minutes late, I was pulling my chair up to my desk. I was extremely proud of myself, and I'd even managed to cover up the jam stain on my dress.

It had to be donut jam; I would bet on it. They were my go-to snack on any occasion and were a major contributor to my curves, of which I had many. I had Double D boobs, hips that swung of their own accord, and a bum that was made for twerking. I did not have the body normally associated with a health and fitness company, but that was who I worked for. Tranter Gyms & Fitness were the biggest franchise of gyms in the country, and I was PA to its CEO, Freddie Tranter. At thirty-four years old and being a six-foot-three hunk of sexiness, Freddie was the man of every girl's dreams. He looked as good in a suit as he did athletic shorts and a training vest. I'd seen him in both, so was well qualified to comment. He wore smart, slim-fitting suits by day, then he slipped into his gym gear every evening to either go down to the gym on the ground floor, or for a run around the city centre. I was convinced that most people who stayed to work after five-thirty were there just to see Freddie in his workout gear.

Talking of sex on legs, there he was coming out of his office, looking down at his phone as he approached my desk. Not in workout gear, but a grey suit and pale-blue shirt with his hair styled to perfection. I didn't think in the year and a half that I'd worked for him I'd ever seen him look anything less than immaculate.

"Morning, Freddie," I chirped as he drew to a stop.

"Natty," he replied without looking up from his phone.

While I waited, I used the time wisely and considered his underwear. It was my regular thing to do when looking at him. Was today a boxer day, boxer-briefs, tighty-whiteys, or maybe he was commando? Now, there was a thought.

Hmm, he was frowning so maybe it was tighty-whiteys and they were a bit too tighty around his huge penis and tremendously sized balls. This I *wasn't* qualified to comment on, but a man that *looked* like him surely couldn't have a penis the size of a barbeque sausage.

"You were late," he suddenly announced, making me jump in my seat.

I looked up to see he was watching me. "Sorry, I overslept."

"Hmm." He was back on his phone for a few seconds before muttering distractedly, "Late night or just couldn't be arsed to get out of bed?"

I thought about it for a few seconds. "I'd say a mixture of both. Sorry, I'll make the time back later."

He frowned. "Don't be stupid. It was six minutes not six hours, and it's not like you do it a lot." He arched a brow. "Unless, of course, that flatmate of yours is having a breakup. You really need to introduce him to some nice girls."

I grinned at his assumption.

"Anyway, I don't have time to arse around. My report—"

"Will be with you by lunchtime," I interrupted, grinning proudly.

"Oh, okay, I was going to say it'll do tomorrow."

I sagged with relief. I really didn't want to have to think about profit margins and costs before I'd had a greasy bacon butty for mid-morning break.

"Also, please can you organise lunch for six people. I've got Chris James coming in at one with his agent about the online fitness show. Sorry, I know it's a last-minute thing, but he called me late last night."

I nodded. "No problem. The usual?"

"Yes please, and include some fruit, I feel like I haven't seen an apple in years."

"Well, you will entertain investors in the evening."

"It's expected of me." He sighed and made a move to leave. At the last minute he turned to me. "And I thought your birthday was in February?"

I followed the line of his finger pointing towards my boob and grinned at the birthday girl badge. When you needed to hide donut jam, what was a girl to do?

CHAPTER TWO

After the manic start to the day, the rest of the morning dragged. Freddie was in his office with 'Do Not Disturb' on his phone, which meant that I had to field calls from his latest 'girlfriend', Bethany. She'd called him four times, on the hour every hour, and I was sure she was convinced that I was lying about him being busy. I was also sure she knew that she was on borrowed time. They'd be seeing each other for almost a month and Freddie's longest relationship that I was aware of was with his dentist. Everyone before her only lasted around the three-to-four-week mark; I was the one who sent the apology bouquet to each of them.

When my phone rang with the outside line, it didn't take a clairvoyant to know it would be her again. It had been fifty-eight minutes since her last call.

"Hi, Bethany," I said without her needing to introduce herself. "He's still in DND, sorry."

"Where the hell is that?" she yelled down the line. "Is it another woman or a club? Where the fuck is he? Is it a new restaurant I don't know about?"

I blinked, stared down at the handset, frowned, and put it back to my ear. "Do not disturb, Bethany. He's in do not disturb mode on his phone."

There was a pause while her brain kicked into gear and she giggled. "What am I like? Sorry, Natty, is he free?"

What did she not understand about the words 'Do not disturb'? "No, Bethany, he's not free. He's busy."

"Still?" She sighed heavily. "I really need to speak to him. Do you think you could disturb him?"

Pinching the bridge of my nose, I looked over at his door which was firmly closed. "No, Bethany, I don't."

"It's important though. One quick minute is all it will take."

The beginning of a headache began to thrum against my temples. I glanced at the time on my computer screen. 12:26. Almost lunchtime. Hanger pains were kicking in and the petite blonde on the other end of the line wasn't helping.

"He's got a lunch meeting at one, but I'll try my very best to speak to him before that." It was a lie. I wouldn't have the opportunity because if I knew anything about Freddie Tranter, it was that he had a toilet schedule. One wee in the morning at 10:45, and two in the afternoon at 12:45 and 16:15 because he had two cups of green tea. Therefore, he'd be weeing during my window of opportunity, and I wasn't about to follow him into the gents to tell him his girlfriend was desperate to speak to him.

"And what time is it now?" Bethany asked.

"Twelve-thirty."

"*Another half an hour before you speak to him? Really?*"

"Yes, Bethany, really."

"Okay, get him to call me then."

And then the line went dead. "Well, thank you, Bethany. Speak later." I thought about not telling Freddie that she'd called but then I wouldn't be a very good PA, would I? Putting the phone back into the cradle I opened a drawer and pulled out my lunchbox, placing it on the desk. Traces of my hangover were still lingering, and I couldn't face the break room.

"Ooh what do you have today?"

I groaned inwardly. "Hey, Michael." I looked up and smiled at our IT guy. He was twenty-two and had a huge crush on me. Tall, blond, and blue-eyed, he was a catch for any girl. Just not this girl. He was nice enough but maybe a little too eager for me.

"Cheese and ham." I smiled at him as I opened up the box. Cheese and ham on brown bread, with real butter, salt and vinegar crisps, and a Penguin. Not a piece of fruit or vegetable in sight. It was the perfect lunch for me, well, apart from the fact that there was no donut involved.

"You really should let me take you out to lunch one of these days."

"I don't know, Michael, I'm not sure it would be a good idea." I flicked the phone to *Do Not Disturb* and lifted one half of my sandwich to my mouth. From the corner of my eye, I caught sight of Michael staring at me as I was about to take a bite. "What?"

He startled then gave me a smile. "I was admiring your lipstick."

"It's the same lipstick that I wear every day, Michael. Charlotte Tilbury Red Carpet." I smiled happily at the idea of the other three that I had at home.

"You smell nice too."

As he moved closer, I leaned back to evade him.

"Your dress is cute, but I didn't know that it was your birthday. I thought that it was February."

I looked down at the badge again. "Donut jam."

Michael laughed and crossed his arms over his chest. "That's funny."

"What's not funny is you're both supposed to be working."

I looked past Michael to see Freddie. He was towering over us with his arms crossed against his chest and his face looked like it had been slapped with a wet fish.

"Why are you here flirting when you should be at your own desk figuring out why the video conferencing equipment isn't working in the boardroom? And you," he said pointing at me, "what have I told you about eating your lunch at your desk?"

"Not to." I took a bite from my sandwich and flashed him a smile. "Eat it in the break room."

"Exactly, so why are you eating at your desk?"

"That would be because I have a very important message for you. I didn't want to miss you."

He raised a perfect brow, waiting for my lie. "And that is?"

"It's from Bethany."

"Bethany?"

"Yes Bethany, she wa—"

He held up his hand. "Hang on a minute." He turned to Michael. "Why are you still hanging around?"

Michael jumped up quickly from his perch on the edge of my desk. "Oh sorry. I'll see you later, Natty." He gave me a look which I think was supposed to be conspiratorial, like we were best buddies who'd been caught out by the teacher, before leaving.

"You do know he's too young for you, don't you?" Freddie asked.

I shrugged. "I don't know, I've never had a younger boyfriend before. It might be a nice change."

"From what, a middle-aged prick with an Audi?"

"I went on two dates with him," I protested. "And he was your client."

"He was not my client. He worked for me. He had a franchise in Crewe." He shoved his hands into his trouser pockets and pushed out his chest. His very broad, very chiselled chest. "That should have told you everything about him."

"What's wrong with Crewe?" I'd never been to Crewe so had no idea what it was like.

"I heard it's a dump."

"You heard?" I shook my head. "You're such a snob, Freddie. And in any case, you're the one who opened a franchise there."

"I didn't, *he* did. He took over an old gym there and approached me for a franchise." He shrugged. "Doesn't mean I think it's a nice place. I just take the money, honey."

I rolled my eyes and took another bite of my sandwich. "Bethany wants to speak to you and has called four time this morning. Every sixty minutes to be precise."

"Fuck," he muttered under his breath. "Could you—"

"Order her some flowers?" I asked, grinning at him.

"Put her through when she calls again and yeah, get the flowers delivered tomorrow."

Saluting him I watched his perfectly tight arse as he wandered back to his office. When he got to the door he paused and turned to me.

"What are you doing on Saturday evening?" he asked.

Nothing. Maybe painting my nails or putting my feet up with a tub of ice cream and watching Casualty. "I have a date, why?"

With his hands still in his pockets, he walked

back to my desk, leaning at the waist to talk into my ear. "Can you postpone it? Only, I need someone to come to a dinner with me."

I looked over my shoulder, glancing towards the main office. No one was listening or even looking in our direction.

"Why are you whispering? Are you afraid someone will say something about you being seen with me?"

It wouldn't be the first time a guy had commented about being seen with a 'big girl'. I had no such qualms about my body. If a guy couldn't see past a few stretch marks and a bit extra around the waist then I didn't want to be seen with them. "Because if that's the case, Freddie, I can honestly say you can shove your job up your tight arse and find yourself someone who fits in to the surroundings better than I do. However, I should point out you won't find anyone as good at the job as I am."

Freddie's face formed into an angry mask as he stood up straight. "How insulting is that?" he demanded. "Do you think I'm that narrow-minded?"

"I didn't think you were, but why else would you be whispering?"

"Because this lot are a nosey bunch of fuckers, and I don't want them knowing my business. Just because you're ginger, Natty, doesn't mean I'd be embarrassed."

"Ginger!" I dropped my sandwich into my lunchbox and grabbed the arms of the chair. "What's wrong with being ginger?"

"Nothing is wrong with being ginger. I thought that you thought that I thought there was. My grandad was ginger, there was a good chance I might have been ginger." He stabbed a finger at his chest. "Any kids I have could be ginger. I'd have been proud to be ginger."

"Well, so am I." I flicked my long *titian* hair over my shoulder. "I thought that you were embarrassed because I'm not exactly skinny."

Freddie frowned and put his hands to his hips. "That's even more disgusting than thinking that I'm embarrassed that you're ginger. When have I ever made any hint that I didn't like your figure? In fact..." His words trailed off and he shook his head. "I am not embarrassed by your figure or your bloody hair colour. I just don't want people putting two and two together and coming up with we're at it like rabbits on my desk at every opportunity."

I gave a quiet gasp at the idea of it because it sounded hot. Quickly pulling myself together I snatched up my bag of crisps.

"I'll come to the dinner with you. Black tie or informal?"

"Black tie," he retorted, shoving his hands back into his pockets. "What about your date? Don't you want to speak to him first?"

"It's fine. It'll be okay." I can eat ice cream any night of the week, mate, don't you worry about that. "I assume there'll be food."

"Yes. It's a four-course dinner, then an auction of stuff that people donate to help with tax relief." He rolled his eyes as he turned and walked away, giving me another view of his bum. "And don't forget the flowers for Bethany and I'm going for a pee."

Then right on cue, the phone rang out and I knew the person on the other end was about to get their ego broken.

CHAPTER THREE

Letting myself into my flat I could practically smell the bottle of rosé which was already open in the fridge. It hadn't been a bad day, just busy trying to fend Bethany off after Freddie dumped her. I even did fast delivery on the flowers, but it didn't have much effect on her. The calls continued, then Jack on the front door called me to say that a blonde woman brandishing a French stick of bread was screaming that Freddie come out to see her.

What the French stick was for, I had no clue. Maybe she was going to clock him over the head with it, knock him out and drag him back to her house. I managed to calm her down and get her into a taxi home, but only because I promised that Freddie would call her later.

So I threw him under the bus. He left me to deal with it by hiding in the stationary cupboard. He said he had no clue that Bethany was there, but I wasn't sure I believed him.

"Andrew, you home?"

There was silence and I gave a tiny sigh of relief. I loved him dearly but sometimes the quiet was more appealing. Going to the fridge I pulled open the door and took out the nice cold bottle. There was a glass on the draining board, so I filled it halfway, kicked off my shoes, and padded to the lounge. Andrew's jumper and a pair of jeans were draped over the chair, and I frowned, not recalling them being there that morning. In fact, weren't they the clothes that he'd put on *that* morning? I picked them up and stared at them, wondering when he'd come home and changed.

I walked towards the bedroom to put the clothes away and when I opened the door, I screamed and jumped about a foot in the air. He was naked and pumping his hips hard as the guy underneath him gripped the duvet and moaned silently, pure ecstasy on his face.

Andrew's head shot up and his eyes were as wide as saucers as he saw me in the doorway.

"You're early?" he grunted mid-thrust.

"No, I'm not but you're clearly too busy to realise the time." I buried my face in his jumper. "I was going to put your clothes back, seeing as you left them in the lounge, you idiot."

"Any chance you could leave?" he asked.

I peeked over the top of the jumper and the guy was looking my way. I gave him a wave and he smiled and sent one back.

"This is Miles."

"Hi Miles. I'm Natty, Andrew's best friend."

"Well, you won't be for much longer if you don't get out."

I suddenly remembered where I was, threw the clothes across the room, and made a swift exit back to my wine.

Andrew and I had been friends since we were five and we'd both known from the age of nine that he was gay. It was when I tried to kiss him at Ava Jacob's birthday party, and he screwed his face up before wiping his mouth. I was mortified and Andrew cried because he'd upset me. When I asked if he thought I was ugly he said no I was very pretty, but he wished I was Bobby Edwards. For the rest of the party, we sat behind the curtains in the dining room and talked about boys. I don't think we knew what gay meant at that age. We'd heard the word and knew it was when men liked kissing men and women liked kissing women, but that was the limit of our nine-year-old knowledge. After that we sneaked on my sister's computer and researched everything we could. Andrew will admit he learned everything he needed to know from the original series of Queer as Folk as we secretly watched it on YouTube whenever my sister went out.

When we both left university the most natural thing was for us to get a flat together. We'd shared a house at uni in Sheffield along with twin sisters Alison and Harriet who had questionable friends. Because of that, Andrew and I often shared a bed, both afraid for our lives. Well, at least our blood. Alison and Harriet took the word Goth to the extreme and both them and their friends had their teeth sharpened to fangs. Every morning we even checked each other's necks for bite marks. It was why we were so comfortable with each other, naked or otherwise. We'd been a team for over twenty years, and nothing would change that. Even catching him having sex with his latest boyfriend.

I took a fortifying drink of wine and dropped onto the sofa, surfing the TV channels to find something to keep me occupied.

Half an hour into an episode of a nature

program, Andrew came into the room in just his jeans and a huge grin.

"You have extremely quiet sex," I said as he sat next to me.

He took the glass from my hand and took a swig. "Doesn't mean it isn't good."

"I know that but it's very weird. You could have at least warned me with a few grunts and groans."

Andrew laughed and nudged me. "Sorry. If I'd realised the time I'd have locked my bedroom door."

"Did you skip work or something?"

He worked as a computer programmer for an IT company that created apps for the financial sector. He earned a huge salary and could easily afford a fancy apartment in the city centre, but he chose to live in a tiny flat above a dress shop with me.

"I had some holiday owing to me. Miles was off so we thought we'd spend the afternoon here."

"God, my life is boring. I spent the afternoon getting rid of Freddie's latest dumpee."

With wide eyes he gasped. "He dumped Bethany? No way! How did that go?"

"She turned up at the office with a French stick."

"Oh okay." He nodded and took the TV remote from me. "It's as good a weapon as any."

"I think she may have been in Tesco when she got the call from him."

"What sort of dick is he that he dumps them via a call?"

"At least it isn't a text." I raised a brow.

"It was just the once and he wouldn't answer my calls." He changed the channel to some quiz show. "Freddie does it all the time."

He was right, he did, but in Freddie's defence, the two that he did dump face to face... one slapped him, and one kneed him in the balls. It was much easier for him via the phone. It wasn't like he promised them anything, like life-long commitment or gold card access to his trillions in the bank.

Yep, Freddie Tranter was worth a hell of a lot of money. He had over ninety of his gyms franchised around the UK, twenty in the US, and didn't need to go into the office every day. He could quite easily sit on a beach in the Bahamas and watch the money roll in. He didn't, though, because he liked to be busy and couldn't stand the thought of his brain getting stagnant.

"It's a good job he's a decent boss," Andrew said.

"He's a nice person who just isn't very good at relationships." When I heard a noise behind us, I turned to see Miles was hovering. "Oh, hi there."

He gave a tentative wave and took a step inside the room. "Sorry about..." He aimed his thumb over his shoulder.

"It's fine." I waved him in. "Come and sit with us."

He looked at Andrew who was grinning at him and made the final few steps to the sofa and sat down.

"Have you thought about dinner?" I asked.

"Pizza," Andrew answered, running his fingers through Miles' messy hair.

"Sounds good to me." I snatched the remote back and turned to the nature programme again. "Talking of dinner and Freddie, he's asked me to go to one with him next week."

"Shut the front door." Andrew stopped messing with Miles' hair mid-stroke. "He did not."

I nodded. "There's an auction, too."

"You have to bid on him? What, so you can have him be your slave for a day or something?"

"No." I scoffed and rolled my eyes. "You bid on items, and it's not like I have the funds to bid on anything, let alone my boss."

"Is he hot?" Miles asked.

I paused, wondering what to say before Andrew answered for me.

"Hot isn't really adequate enough to describe him. He's like hot to the power of twenty. Oh, and Natty has a little crush on him."

"I do not." I laughed and fixed my gaze onto the television. "He's gorgeous, but he's my boss. And he has issues with relationships that last longer than the bottle of hand sanitiser that he has on his desk."

"And yet you've been in a relationship with him for almost eighteen months."

"I work for him. I'm not in a relationship with him."

"It's a relationship of sorts," Andrew replied, trying unsuccessfully to get the remote from me again. "It's the best one he's ever had and now..." he grinned at me. "And now you're going on a date. I'm so proud of you." He chuckled and rubbed my hair.

I swatted him away. "You bloody idiot. And I told you it's a work thing, it's not a date."

"Whatever you say, love. Right," he slapped my thigh and gave a quick kiss to Miles' cheek before standing up. "I'm guessing it's pepperoni for you, Natty."

Dickhead.

CHAPTER FOUR

"Natty, get in here, would you!"

I groaned, it was coffee and donut time and now Freddie wanted me in his office. He sounded stressed so that meant I'd probably be in there for bloody ages while he ranted on about something.

I picked up my iPad and tottered in as fast as I could in a tight pencil skirt and my charity shop Gianvito Rossi Plexi Pumps. Oh, and let me tell you, when your skirt was as tight as mine, chub-rub shorts were a must. No one wanted to walk around all day with stinging inner thighs.

"Hey," I said, pushing the door closed behind me. "You called."

Freddie's head rose from the papers on his desk

and when his eyes landed on me he blinked slowly.

"You okay?" I asked.

"What?"

"Are *you* okay?"

He gave his head a little shake, like a dog with a bee buzzing around its ear. "No. Yeah. Yep. I'm great."

"So, what did you want me for?"

He watched me walk across to his visitor chair and drop myself into it. When I crossed my legs and rested the iPad on my lap he finally answered. "I need you to organise some hotel rooms. There's a Japanese guy and his business partner coming over next week. They're considering setting up several franchises over there. I've emailed you the dates and names."

People often asked what was so good about Tranter gyms. Not only was Freddie extremely competitive in his franchise fee, but his gyms also had a loyalty membership. The more times you worked out, the more points you earned. At the end of every year the points were converted to cash. Either off the following year's membership or merchandise with the Tranter logo on it. He also ensured every single franchise owner abided by his rules for their gym.

"Just the two of them?"

"No, they're bringing their wives so two double rooms. Get them into Malmaison, if you can. Three nights, plus return flights whatever the quickest route is for them." He cleared his throat and scratched the back of his neck. "Tell accounts that I've cleared it."

"Do you want me to organise anything for them while they're here? Maybe the horse racing, or a football game?"

He shook his head. "No, they're coming midweek before going onto London on the Friday, so get the flights back from Heathrow. Book dinner on the second night at *Tast Catala*. I'll take them with Jacob."

Jacob was Freddie's best friend and his Financial Director. They met in sixth form at high school and Freddie came up with the idea of the gym then. He'd always said he didn't think that he'd actually do it, but when he was twenty his grandad died and left him enough money to buy an old, clapped-out gym in his home town. It was the first Tranter Gym and within three years he had five in total and was able to employ Jacob full time. Now, fourteen years later he had...well, now he was a multi-millionaire.

"Talking of Jacob, why don't you take him with

you to the dinner and auction?" I asked, watching him carefully. Jacob was always his wingman.

"He's away for the weekend. Rebecca wants a break before the baby comes. They're going to a fancy spa." Freddie turned back to the papers on his desk and shifted them around. "Do you have a copy of the building regs for the new build in Oxford?"

"A hard copy?"

He shifted in his seat and rubbed a hand over his mouth. "Yep."

"I left one on your desk yesterday." I sat up and leaned closer to the desk, peering at it. "What the hell have you been doing?"

There were papers everywhere. Not to mention a whole load of sweet wrappers.

"Why, Freddie Tranter, you're a secret sweet eater. You naughty boy."

"I was here late and was hungry."

"And you of all people, should know green tea and Werther's are not a balanced diet."

His cheeks pinked and he looked suitably chastised, which was very cute.

"I just need the damn paper, Natty, and I can't find it."

Sighing, I stood up and moved around to his side of the desk. Leaning over him I rifled through the mayhem. At first I wasn't aware at exactly how close we were, but when he moved his chair back his shoulder brushed against my boob. It might have been the fact that it had been almost eight months since a man had touched me. Or it *might* have been the fact that it was Freddie who was touching me. Okay, it was just his shoulder, and he probably hadn't done it intentionally, but there was a definite stirring behind the lace of my bra.

Freddie quickly put more distance between us. "It's on there somewhere." His voice was rough.

I had no idea why, but I could barely catch my breath. I was practically panting as I moved papers around. There was even a tremor to my hands as I put his desk into some sort of order, piling papers and brushing sweet wrappers into his waste bin. Finally finding what I was looking for, I picked it up and turned to Freddie. As I did, he jumped because I knew, without doubt, I'd caught him looking at my bum.

Well, that was a turn up for the books. I mean, my bum did look good in the skirt that I was wearing but I'd never expect Freddie to think so. Maybe he was looking at it and thinking it could do with a few sessions in one of his gyms?

Personally, I thought it was a great arse, but not

the sort of great arse that I expected Freddie to spend time perusing. Nevertheless, a little buzz went through my body at the possibilities.

"Here you go." I handed the paper to him and maybe leaned over a little further than necessary. I was a woman who liked men to look at her and my boobs looked amazing in my bra. Even if he did only get a glimpse at the curve of them down my cream silk blouse. When he swallowed, I bit on my bottom lip to stop myself from smiling. It appeared that maybe I was right, and my hot boss did have a tiny crush on my bum and boobs. Well, that was interesting.

"Anything else?" I asked, picking my iPad up, my breaths still coming in short pants.

"No, erm, that's fine thanks."

"Okay, I'll get this all sorted." I admit that when I walked to the door I swung my hips a little more than usual. That was why I had them after all.

The door handle was in my palm when Freddie spoke. "Hey, Natty."

"Yes." I turned back to him with the sweetest of smiles.

"Do you need a dress for the dinner? Because if you do, you can take the company credit card. I mean, it's a working function, so it would only be fair."

I shook my head and sighed. "Freddie, do I look like the kind of woman who doesn't have a dress for every occasion?"

The way his eyes studied me, and his chest went up and down in short, sharp breaths it was like he was seeing me for the first time. After over a year we were *both* seeing each other for the first time. In an entirely different way than boss and employee.

While it would never mean anything other than a little workplace flirtation, it was a good feeling to have. To be desired and looked at.

"No," Freddie said, his voice breaking into my thoughts. "I would imagine you had an outfit for any type of occasion."

"Exactly," I replied. "So don't worry, I won't embarrass you with a cheap and nasty dress."

He sat back in his chair and ran a hand over his face, like he was warring with himself over something.

"No, Natty," he sighed. "I never thought you would."

With that I gave him a wink and sashayed my way out of there, and maybe my lacey knickers were a little damp.

CHAPTER FIVE

M y week leading up to the dinner and auction was mundane to say the least. Work and no play whatsoever. In fact, it was quite boring seeing as Freddie had meetings in Glasgow. He'd called earlier in the day to tell me he'd pick me up at six-thirty. I'd told him I could meet him at the venue, but he'd been insistent.

"What do you think?" I asked Andrew as he stir fried vegetables in a wok.

He cocked his head to one side and perused me. After a few seconds his face broke into a soft smile. "You look beautiful, love."

"Are you sure?" It wasn't that I was insecure. I was what I was. However, I didn't have oodles of self-assurance to the point I was blind.

My dress was long, red velvet, low at the front and hugged my curves.

I was a bombshell. The kind painted on the side of a war plane.

"I like your hair like that."

I touched the long loose curls that framed my face and grinned. "I was going for film star after a heavy night. Did I succeed?"

"I think you look a little better put together than that, darling, but you do look amazing." He removed the wok from the heat and moved over to me, pulling me into a hug. "You're going to be the sexiest woman there."

"I don't know about that. There are going to be models, TV stars and a couple of popstars there tonight." I was confident, though. Carrying a bit of extra timber maybe, but the way I looked at it, there was so much more of me to go around.

"Will Freddie be wearing a tux?" Andrew asked, fluttering his eyelashes. "Ooh imagine that." He went back to his cooking, humming as he stirred the contents of the wok.

I had. Often.

"I presume so." I opened my clutch bag and pulled out my mirror to check my lipstick. Smacking my lips, happy that it was still perfect, I turned to Andrew. "I'm off then."

He looked over his shoulder. "Is he picking you up?"

"I said I'd meet him outside."

"Have fun."

With butterflies fluttering around in my stomach, I let myself out of the flat to wait outside for my lift.

When I stepped onto the pavement, I gasped. Parked at the side of the road was a sleek, black, limousine. I was sure that it must be Freddie, but you never knew when a random limo would park outside your house. Look at Julia Roberts, I bet when she went out for work that night she didn't expect Richard Gere to ask her to drive his car. Even so, Richard Gere aside, I hoped I didn't look like a prostitute. I'd have to give quite a few handies to afford the dress I was wearing that was for sure.

Looking at the car and wondering whether to approach it, I jumped when the back door opened. A long leg in black trousers appeared first, then the rest of the body. As Freddie straightened, my knees *actually* knocked together – surprising seeing as I always thought that was a myth.

You know when you see those men in aftershave

adverts? The ones who give you real flutters in your knickers. Well, Freddie was like one of those. Tall, his hair styled perfectly, except for a couple of strands which fell in front of his forehead. He had the right amount of stubble and a gorgeous slim-fitting tux. He didn't wear one of those stupid dickie bows but a thin black tie which was loosely knotted. All he needed to do was look down the lens of the camera and say in a deep voice, 'Stag, the cologne for men who really know how to give head'.

"Hey." Feeling breathless, I gave him a wave, seeing as I couldn't move my legs.

"Wow." Holding onto the limo door, Freddie didn't move either but shoved his hand into his trouser pocket. "You look, amazing."

The sincerity in his voice made me feel a little emotional. I had never, ever had a crisis of confidence about who I was. That didn't stop other people finding it necessary to give their opinion though. When I was complimented it was often things like, you're actually quite pretty, or don't they do lovely clothes in bigger sizes, or my personal favourite, you don't sweat much for a fat girl, do you? So, for Freddie to tell me that I looked amazing and not clarify it with a statement about my size was enough to make me want to cry.

"Thank you." I sucked in a breath to stem the stupid girly tears. "So do you."

He rolled his eyes and waved a hand at me. "Aww shucks."

Giggling, I took the couple of steps to stand in front of him, glad that my legs were working again. "Hi."

"Hi," he said softly. "You ready for this?"

"I don't know, will there be ice cream for dessert?"

He grinned and shrugged. "I don't know. There will be dessert, so it could possibly be ice cream."

"Well then I'm ready."

Freddie stood to one side so I could get in the car. Once I was sitting he leaned inside with one hand on the door. "I'll go round the other side."

"That's good because now I'm sitting down this dress is a little tight. I'm not sure I have much scooching room in it."

Freddie scrubbed a hand over his mouth and muttered a 'yep', before closing the door.

As we walked into the venue my breath stalled. I didn't think I'd seen anything more beautiful, except maybe Freddie in his tux. There were thousands of bare white bulbs strung across the expanse of the ceiling, huge vases of white roses and lilies were placed strategically around the room and soft music played. It was like a fairy tale and with my hand tucked in the crook of Freddie's arm, I felt like a princess. Okay, maybe more a brunette Jessica Rabbit, but it was still magical.

"It's beautiful."

Freddie tutted. "Waste of damn money if you ask me. We're here for charity, so why not spend the cash people pay to be here on the *charity*. Or is that too obvious?"

He had a point. "Yes, you're right, but you have to admit it does look gorgeous."

"Come on, let's get a drink to help us through this shit show."

I tugged on his arm. "Oh, stop being a grump and let me get you a slippery nipple."

"That fucking bloke hasn't stopped looking at your arse," Freddie grumbled half an hour later as he necked the last of his champagne. "He's a dirty perv."

I almost choked on the bubbles, recalling a certain man also looking at my arse a few days before. "Why is he a perv just because he's looking at my bum?" I looked over my shoulder and flashed a smile at the guy in question. "Maybe he just appreciates the finer things in life."

Freddie blew out his cheeks and a smirk twitched at his lips. "It *is* pretty fine."

Smiling behind the rim of my glass I tried not to squeal with excitement. Who knew if it was the champagne talking or whether he did think I had fine arse? It didn't matter because I liked that he'd said it.

I was a woman who liked compliments and if he wanted to hang from some scaffolding, wolf-whistle, and shout, 'nice arse, darling', then that was fine with me.

"Looks like the auction is about to start," Freddie said, nudging me.

Someone was hauling a podium onto the stage while a grey-haired guy looked down at a piece of paper.

"Are you one of the prizes?" I asked.

Freddie frowned. "You read far too many of those dirty books."

"What's that got to do with it?"

"Don't they always have a part where the guy is auctioned off, and the girl wins a date with him, then they end up shagging in a lift?"

I blinked slowly. "For someone who claims never to have read a romance book, you seem to be very intimate with the plot."

"You're always telling me about them, that's how I know." As a waiter passed, Freddie grabbed two more glasses of champagne. "You'll want this, these fucking auctions go on for hours."

I turned and tapped the same waiter on the shoulder. "Two more please." I twisted and gave one to Freddie. "Don't get too pissed and bid for something ridiculous like sheep shearing in Wales."

Freddie snorted. "If I do then you're coming with me."

I laughed and grabbed hold of his arm. "Come on, let's go back to our table and get you that trip to Wales."

Forty minutes later, the auction was in full swing. It had started with some minor items like picnic baskets, a meat hamper and a family ticket to a theme park. I hadn't bid on anything. I didn't have the money for starters but, also, I was feeling pretty squiffy. I was sure the alcohol along with my burning desire to win would have resulted in me spending my life savings on a few pork chops and some chipolatas.

"It's the bigger items now," Freddie whispered. He leaned in close and when his lips tickled against my ear, my whole body shivered.

"Okay." I slowly blew out a breath, trying to regulate my heartbeat. The alcohol wasn't the only thing heating my blood.

I was not a girl who was prone to excitement or girly squealy moments, but when Freddie put his arm along the back of my chair, I did consider it. Who would blame me if I jumped on my chair and fist pumped? My boss looked like a walking advert of beautiful manliness, and he was clearly interested in me. I wasn't going to get carried away, though, men could be a fickle beast where women were concerned.

"Freddie. Is that you?"

We both turned away from the stage towards the sultry voice. Like a cross between the good-looking Kardashian and Ariana Grande, there was a woman worthy of a magazine cover. The shimmering green dress she wore caught the light, twinkling in all the right places, and her dark hair was pulled over one tanned shoulder. She was beautiful.

"Carla!" Freddie pushed up out of his chair and

grabbed her into a strong hug. "How the hell are you?"

When they were still entangled after forty seconds – okay, I counted, so shoot me – I was starting to get a little twitchy. When it was clear the next auction item was coming up it was a great excuse to interrupt, and I pulled on Freddie's jacket.

He pulled away from Carla and turned to me. "Sorry, this is Natty, my PA."

Okay, we were back to being boss and PA. It was true and shouldn't have stung, but it did.

"No, no," I protested. "It was just to let you know the next item is starting."

Freddie looked at the stage. "Oh shit."

I expected him to tell Carla he'd see her later before sitting back down.

He didn't.

Instead, he pointed to the bar and said, "I'll be back in a bit."

To say I was deflated was an understatement. I watched him lead Carla away with a hand on the small of her back, just above her bum, which was *pretty fine.* I knew I was being stupid, but a lump formed in my throat, and the prickle of *stupid* tears stung my eyes. Swallowing them and the lump back, I turned to the stage and pulled my shoulders back.

"Can I sit here?"

I whipped my head around. "Oh, hello."

It was the guy who'd been looking at my arse. He was fairly good looking. Blond, not my usual type, he had an earring, again not my thing, but he had a lovely smile. All wide and white teeth.

"Can I?"

I looked at the empty chair before swinging my gaze to the bar. Freddie and Carla were still chatting, and she had her hand on his arm.

"Yes, sure."

He thrust his hand out. "Tim."

"Natty," I replied giving it a shake. "Nice to meet you."

"You, too. I spotted you earlier, but I think you know that." He winked at me and ran his tongue along his bottom teeth.

Any attraction that I might have had immediately disappeared. I had the ick and my champagne was in danger of coming back. I felt bilious as my nan used to say. It was such a good word. Much better than pukey or nauseous, which always made me think of Vikings and longboats for some reason.

"You got your eye on anything in particular?" I asked, nodding to the stage.

43

Of course, I'd set it up for him. What an idiot.

Schoolgirl error, Natty!

"Your arse, obviously."

And twenty points for originality does not go to Tim.

"No," I said with a very small, very minute, laugh. "The auction."

"Are you on offer?"

Oh my god, he was getting worse. "No." I moved my chair so that I put my back to him. Subtlety was not something I imagined Tim understood. I was right because he planted his chin on my shoulder, like a dog wanting his nose scratched.

"How about we get out of here and I get a closer look at that amazing arse of yours?"

"How about you fuck off?" a deep, angry voice said, very loudly.

Freddie was towering over us with two glasses of champagne and the face of a man who had found a dickhead sitting in his seat.

"What?" Tim asked, looking a little confused.

"I said," Freddie leaned in closer, "fuck off. That's my seat."

"You weren't here, mate."

"And now I am." He handed me one of the

glasses of champagne and turned back to Tim. "Do you need me to say it again?"

He narrowed his eyes on Tim and waited. It didn't take long before the seat was vacated, and Freddie was back in it.

"Dickhead," he muttered before turning his attention to the auction. "What item is this?"

"Spa day. I thought you were at the bar with Carla."

"Yeah, we had a quick catch up and now she's gone back to her table." He took a sip of champagne and nodded at the stage. "You fancy it?"

I looked at the stage and then back at Freddie. "Not really, no. Why?"

"I'd have bid on it for you if you did."

"Did Carla give you drugs, prescription or otherwise, while you were over there?"

"Shush," he said. "The bidding has started and if you don't want it I might get it for my mum."

"Okay." I shifted my chair a little closer to him. "So is Carla an ex?" I asked. "Or an old friend?"

"Old friend," he whispered from the corner of his mouth. "And just so you know, she wanted to know if you were single." He grinned and winked and when he did it, it was so much sexier than Tim.

"What? Me?"

"Oh yeah," he replied with a little smirk. "She was very interested and wanted to invite you out for dinner."

"And what did you say?" I could feel a little blush rising over my cleavage. I'd never had a woman interested in me before. I wasn't sure how to handle it.

Freddie put his arm along the back of my chair again, but this time his thumb rubbed gently up and down on my shoulder.

"I told her that I'd give you her number."

"Oh, okay." That was a little disappointing.

"However, I did tell her not to get her hopes up," he whispered.

"Why? I mean I'm not gay, but I might like to go to dinner with her. If only to ask how she gets her makeup looking so great."

"Maybe," he replied. "But once I've taken you to a proper dinner I don't think anyone else will get a look in."

"A *proper dinner*. What's that exactly?" I asked, unable to stop myself from grinning.

"Well," he said, leaning in close, his breath whispering against my skin. "A proper dinner is where we aren't surrounded by a hundred other people. Where we eat the best food and drink the best wine, not like the processed crap we just had. And," he said, moving in closer, "a dinner where *no one* will interrupt us or our plans for the evening and throughout the night."

His tone was low, full of sexy innuendo and all I could do was push my thighs together and swig back the champagne. The bubbles took my breath away making me splutter until Freddie's gentle patting of my back stopped me from choking.

"Sorry, it went down the wrong way."

"Are you okay now?" He rubbed circles on my back, and warmth flooded through me.

"I'm fine, thanks."

"Good. So, that's okay, then? If I take you to a proper dinner?"

Unable to speak, I just nodded.

"Excellent," Freddie said as he tapped my knee. "Now, watch the auction because I have to see if there's any sheep shearing."

CHAPTER SIX

In the back of the limo, I was second guessing whether he meant what he said about dinner. He hadn't mentioned it again, not even when there had been a champagne dinner for two prepared by a top chef in the winner's own kitchen. I thought he might bid on it, but he didn't. He did win the spa day for his mum, though.

Feeling uncomfortable in the silence, I cleared my throat and sighed. I opened my mouth and closed it again. I took a deep breath and blew it out.

"What's wrong?" Freddie asked.

I whipped my head in his direction to see he was grinning. "What's so funny?"

He shook his head. "Nothing. I'm just

wondering why you're acting like a nervous teenager on a first date."

"No, I'm not," I protested. "And anyway, this isn't a date."

He arched an eyebrow. "Yet you're acting like a teenager on one." He looked down at his phone and tapped at the screen.

His fingers were long and slim, but not too dainty that they looked like women's. In fact, they looked like they could perform amazing magic. As I daydreamed about them, he dropped his phone on the seat between us.

"Is this about us going to dinner?" He turned towards me so that his knees touched mine. "If you don't want to go, you don't have to. I'm not going to hold it against you. Is that what you thought?"

"God, no." I didn't know what to say to him. How did I explain that I did feel like a teenager? Or that in the last three hours my appreciation of his good looks had turned from good old horny attraction to full on crush? "I do want to go. I know you wouldn't hold it against me."

"So?" He grabbed my hand and pulled it to him, putting it between both his large, warm palms. It was nice. "Natty, talk to me."

God, this was all so weird.

"Why did you ask me out to dinner, Freddie? You've never shown any interest in me before."

"I have," he argued. "I know your best friend is Andrew and he has poor taste in women."

"How do you know that?" I held back a smile.

"Because," he said on a sigh, "if he had good taste in women he'd have made sure you were his a long time ago. Fuck being best mates."

I started to giggle. He actually looked angry. "You're such an idiot."

"What? Why? You're fucking stunning. You're funny and bright. Why the hell wouldn't he want you?"

Freddie's hands squeezed mine tighter and his eyes softened.

God, he was beautiful.

"He's gay, that's why," I replied, my voice barely above a whisper because I was still gazing at him.

"Gay!"

I nodded. "Yep. He's seeing a really nice guy called Miles."

"Why the hell didn't you tell me that?"

"Because it wasn't necessary. You don't know him other than he's my best friend and that I live with him."

"And that's why he's never asked you out?"

"Er yeah." I shrugged. "And the fact that we've known each other since we were five."

"Wow." He scratched his head. "That's blown my mind."

"Oh, don't be so ridiculous."

I missed the feel of his hand on top of mine. I had to force myself not to grab it back from his thigh, where he was now resting it.

"It explains so much," Freddie said.

"But not why you suddenly want to take me on a date."

At that moment the limo lost control and we found ourselves being thrown around. Freddie braced against the door, grabbing my hand as I was jostled backwards and forwards, landing with my face in his chest.

"Shit. Are you okay?" He leaned forward and banged on the privacy panel. "Oi, drive more carefully."

The panel came down and the driver held up a hand. "Sorry sir. A couple of drunken girls walked out into the middle of the road. I apologise, Miss."

"It's fine," I said, even though it was muffled as I was still plastered to Freddie's chest.

When the panel went back up, he gently lifted

my chin and looked down at me. "Are you sure you're okay?"

"Yes. Honestly."

Except for the fact that my nipples hurt and there was a pulsing between my legs which was *really* annoying.

Freddie took in a deep breath and wet his lips. "Natty, I really like you. I've liked you for a long time. You always brighten up my day."

"Really?" I laughed. "You always seem so grumpy."

"I do?" He frowned. "That's my happy demeanour."

"Okay, but why ask me on a date?" I pushed away from his chest and grimaced. "It was a date right, not just dinner?"

"It's a date I've asked you on, Natty." He cupped my cheek. "I've wanted to ask you for a long time now, and well tonight seemed to be the right time to ask you."

"How long?" I asked, stunned.

"About six months. Actually, I've fancied you for about nine, but only thought about asking you on a date for six."

My eyes widened on him and when my mouth dropped open, Freddie closed it with a finger under my chin and grinned.

"A shock?"

"Yes a bloody, shock." An absolute bloody shock. Nine months! "I had no idea."

"I'm very good at hiding my feelings."

"No shit, Watson."

"It's Sherlock."

"What is? Who's Sherlock."

"For fuck's sake." With a huge grin, he shook his head. "It's no shit, *Sherlock*."

I frowned at him. "My nanna told me it was Watson."

"Well, your nanna was wrong. I promise you, it's Sherlock."

He was probably right. Nanna was convinced that EastEnders was a reality TV show after all.

"Listen, Natty," Freddie said. "I would like to take you on a date because I'm so attracted to you it's unbelievable. Now, do you want to go or not?"

Of course I wanted to go. "What if we hate each other, or you eat with your mouth open? What about Bethany?"

"We won't and I don't. You've seen me eat plenty of times. Did I ever show you what I was eating?" He sighed. "As for Bethany, a distraction because I was trying to forget about you. In fact, so were Vicki, Sacha, and Josie."

I narrowed my eyes thinking about it. As I did a voice came over a speaker.

"Mr Tranter, we're at Miss Jacob's home."

Silently Freddie cursed and looked at the roof of the limo, before bringing his intense gaze back to me. He didn't say anything, but it was like I could read his mind.

"Andrew is home."

Without a pause Freddie said, "Go to my home address, please." He looked at me questioningly, and I nodded. "Just so you know," he said whispering in my ear, "I have donuts."

I wasn't totally sure what going back to Freddie's house would mean, but I was more than happy to find out. And, if sex didn't happen then maybe I'd get my favourite snack.

CHAPTER SEVEN

I knew that Freddie would live somewhere nice, but his apartment – it was worthy of so much more than the word flat – wasn't exactly what I was expecting. It was so... grown up. There was even a pan in the sink which showed that he actually cooked with them, and they weren't simply for show. The kitchen was black with rose gold taps and accessories, and it smelled of coffee.

My only thought was why had he led me past the lounge where there was a huge, comfy sofa?

"A hot drink or alcohol?" Freddie asked with his hand on the fridge door.

I shrugged. "Whatever you fancy."

The flirtation and fun of the limo was gone, and it seemed like we both felt like teenagers on a date.

Freddie kept glancing at me when he thought that I wasn't looking and every time he did I wanted to giggle.

He raised an eyebrow and shook his head.

"What?" I asked.

"Nothing. Nothing at all." He opened the fridge door and took out a couple of bottles of beer. He passed one to me then pulled out the stool opposite mine and sat down.

"Do you have a bottle opener?" I held up the bottle.

"Shit, sorry." He reached for a drawer in the island and scrambled around. "Where the hell is it?"

As he stretched, his dress shirt came out of the waistband of his trousers and gave me a glimpse of his skin. It was only a tiny amount, but it made my heart thud like a jack hammer. Licking my lips, I pushed my thighs together to try and ease the ache.

"Here it is." He sat upright and took the beer from my hand before flipping the caps on both bottles. "I really need to sort that bloody drawer out." He sighed and lifted his bottle to his lips.

"Everyone has one like that." I laughed. "You should see my drawers."

Freddie coughed, reared forward and spat out his

beer, narrowly missing me as it went over my shoulder.

"Oh my god," he spluttered. "I'm so sorry." Swiping a hand across his chin he groaned. "I'm such a dickhead."

"Did it go down the wrong way?"

"No, Natty, it didn't." He scrubbed a hand down his face. "You can't say things like that."

"What did I say?" I took a large swig of beer, feeling the need to concentrate on something other than Freddie's eyes, and his lips, and his earlobes, and his... I was most definitely obsessed and getting more obsessed with each minute.

"You mentioned your drawers, Nat."

I frowned. "And?"

"Drawers, knickers," he leaned forward and when his face was inches from mine, the room suddenly felt small and airless. "You get it?"

I nodded and swallowed back the groan as I got a waft of his aftershave mixed with the smell of beer. There was something heady and sexy about it. Something that made me want to lean across the granite island, grab his tie and land my lips on his.

"Yeah," I replied breathily. "I get it."

Putting his bottle down, Freddie took a deep breath. "What are we going to do?"

"About?"

He pointed between us. "This. Me and you."

I shrugged. "I don't know, Freddie, because I have no idea what this is. Apart, from me being your PA that is."

"I'm glad I'm not the only one confused."

When he reached for my hand, I had to stop myself from gasping. It was like approaching a stray dog and not wanting to make a sound that might spook it. If I made a noise that brought him back to his senses I'd never forgive myself. If I stayed quiet maybe the little puppy would give me a welcoming lick.

"I can't stop thinking about you, Natty," he said, his voice gravelly. "Since the minute you came to work in that damn pink dress with love hearts all over it."

I frowned, thinking back to when I'd worn the dress. "That was last summer."

"Yep. Like I said, nine months ago."

Nine months, he really did like me, like that, for nine months.

"You looked," he blew out his cheeks, "fucking sexy as hell and I couldn't keep my eyes off you." Dropping his head, Freddie groaned. "I sound like a right weirdo, don't I?"

"Nope." It was all I could think of to say. It was all I could *manage* to say. My heart was beating so fast I could barely catch my breath.

"I'm not, I swear, and I didn't ever perv over you before then, but that fucking dress, Natty." He let go of my hand, stood up, and strode to the opposite side of the kitchen. "I have never even looked at anyone who has worked for me before."

"I don't think you're a perv, Freddie."

He shoved his hands into the pockets of his black tuxedo trousers and lifted his gaze to mine. "You don't?"

"No. Not at all. Quite the opposite." I exhaled slowly. "I just wish I'd known. I'd have worn that dress more often."

He crossed the space between us so fast he was like a blur. I hardly had time to put my bottle of beer down before his hands were at the back of my head. Pulling me to him, he threaded his fingers in my hair and when our lips met he gave a groan, deep from his chest. Grabbing his shoulders, I used him to help pull myself from my stool so that his body was against the full length of mine.

On my tiptoes, arching against Freddie, I pressed my groin against his dick which was rock hard behind his perfectly tailored trousers. One of his hands moved from my hair, trailing down my body until it landed on my arse, and he gave it a squeeze.

"Fuck, Natty."

"Too much talking," I muttered as my mouth sought his again.

With a chuckle, Freddie cupped my face with one hand but when his other left my buttock, I slapped a hand over the top, wanting to keep it exactly where I liked having it. When he then moved it down my leg and pulled at the velvet of my dress, I was more than happy with the change of venue.

"As much as I love this dress," Freddie groaned. "It needs to come off."

It was tight and there was little likelihood of him getting it over my hips. "Zip," I said with a gasp as his lips went to my neck.

"Bedroom."

"Okay."

With my hand in Freddie's, I was dragged from the room, and along a hallway into the room full of promise.

CHAPTER EIGHT

I didn't spend any time checking the room out, other than noting where the bed was. To be fair, I didn't have the opportunity because as soon as we were in there, Freddie resumed where he'd left off in the kitchen. This time, though, his hand immediately went to the zip at the back of my dress. Frenziedly, we both pushed the dress down until it fell around my feet in a pool of red velvet.

Freddie's hands went back to my body, touching, stroking, and pulling while I tugged at his belt. Breathing heavily, I pushed him back a step.

"Get naked."

Freddie grinned and with his hand on my hip, guiding me backwards until I hit the bed.

"Sit."

I did as he asked, full of anxious anticipation at what he was going to do. He leaned in close and kissed me, long and luxuriously, ending it with a nip to my lip. When he straightened, he exhaled and ran a finger down my cheek.

"You're so fucking sexy, Nat."

I loved how he had started to call me Nat. Like it was his special nickname for me because no one else ever used it. I was Natty to everyone, everyone except Freddie.

He stared at me, his gaze penetrating as he pulled his shirt from his trousers and slowly began to unbutton it. When he shrugged it from his body, my clit began to throb, and my desire flowed from me. His body was sculpted with each muscle clearly defined and all I could think of was running my tongue over them. The thought made my nipples so hard they hurt.

When Freddie's hands went to his belt, I inhaled sharply. His concentration was fully on me as he deftly unbuckled it and undid his trousers. Slowly lowering the zip, he wet his lips, swallowing as his hands went inside his boxer-briefs.

"I'm so fucking hard."

Instinctively, I opened my legs and arched my back, desperate to touch myself but wanting to prolong the anticipation. Freddie's eyes were hooded as they lowered, like he could read my mind. I was so wet I was sure that he could see my desire on my knickers. When he grabbed his dick and pumped it, I let out a little moan and Freddie smiled. He kicked off his shoes and socks, while we watched each other. Under his spell, I memorised the sight of him. Who knew what would happen the next day, or the days after that, but if this was to be a one-off then I wanted to remember every single moment. Maybe, we should have taken things slower and thought about the consequences, but we were adults. We would deal with it. I would deal with anything if it meant I got to have sex with Freddie.

The sound of his trousers hitting the floor got my attention and my heartbeat sped up. The air was full of expectancy. It was electric and my adrenalin was feeding off it, racing around my body and lighting me up like a beacon.

When I looked at Freddie in his tight black boxer-briefs, I moved to stand but he held up his hand.

"Wait."

"*Freddie.*"

"Patience, Nat."

Pouting, I sat on my hands to stop myself from

reaching out for him. He grinned as he hooked his thumbs into his waistband and finished getting himself naked. As he dragged the jersey fabric over his rock hard cock, I had a feeling it would only take one touch from him for me to explode.

How could one man look so perfect? It was like a group of women had described the body of their dreams and come up with Freddie. Every man I'd read about in the romance books I loved always seemed to be too perfect, too unattainable, yet here he was.

When he moved towards me, I gasped hoping I was ready for his cock. Thank God it wasn't enormous, but it was still a good size. My main worry was him, Freddie. His demeanour told me he knew exactly how to treat a woman and make her fall apart. He would have the ability to ruin me.

When Freddie moved between my legs and leaned into my space, I held my breath, only expelling it when he dropped a soft kiss to my shoulder. His hand came to my breast, his thumb rubbing across my nipple, sending a shiver throughout my body. With his lips making a slow path along my neck, I moaned softly and opened my legs wider. Freddie put his hand on my hip and pushed his fingers inside my knickers.

"This underwear is unbelievable," he whispered.

I silently congratulated myself on picking the red lace underwear which was the exact same colour as my dress. The bra pushed my boobs up so that I had *the* most amazing cleavage. The knickers were a thong back but were high waisted, covering my stomach which was by no means flat. It was rounded and I had wide hips, more than a little padding on my arse, and my boobs probably wouldn't pass the pencil test, yet the way Freddie's hands were stroking my skin and his lips were caressing my body, I felt sexier than I ever had before. My confidence was sky high as he clearly revered everything single inch of me.

When his hand went down the front of my knickers I almost yelled with excitement. I was desperate, so ready for what he was about to give to me.

A long finger dipped into my wetness, parting my lips, and when he slicked my arousal over my clit I gripped the duvet underneath me. Freddie added another finger and the feeling of ecstasy washed over me like a swathe of silk covering my body. As he pumped, I thrust my hips in time with his rhythm and the burn in the pit of my stomach was growing rapidly.

"Freddie, I need..."

I didn't finish my sentence because Freddie's mouth went to my nipple and sucked it hard over the lace of my bra. It was pleasure and pain. It was amazing. My fingertips dug into his back as I desperately tried to get closer.

"I need to fuck you," Freddie growled as he pulled away from me and his hands went to the waistband of my knickers.

I sat up and reached behind for the clasp of my bra while my underwear was pulled down my legs. Throwing my bra to one side, I watched Freddie as he dropped red lace to the floor at his feet. I shifted up the bed and waited as he reached for his bedside drawer and pulled out a box of condoms. Every move he made was quick and efficient, even pulling a condom out of the box, ripping it open and rolling it down his beautiful cock. Each muscle moved with fluidity, rippling seductively and enticing me to want to explore them more.

When Freddie grabbed my hips and hauled me closer to him, I squealed with delight at his masculinity. I was a woman who wanted to be thrown around, but as a bigger girl it wasn't always possible. Freddie, though, had no problem.

"You want this?" he asked, his teeth nipping at my earlobe.

"God yes." I craned my neck so I could capture his mouth, but he smirked and moved his head back.

"You sure? Because this changes everything, Nat."

It did. I knew it would, but life was too short to regret what you didn't do.

"I'm sure," I rushed out, desperate for the action to begin. "I know things will change and I can deal with it. We can deal."

"Thank fuck, because if I don't get inside of you soon I'll explode."

"Do it. Fuck me."

With one thrust, Freddie's beautiful cock entered me with such force I was shifted up the bed. He pushed my arms above my head and his hand grabbed both my wrists, pinning them to the mattress. Freddie's other hand went to my leg and pushed it up towards my chest, opening me wider as he drilled into me, fast and hard. When he lowered his head and scraped his teeth over my nipple, I screamed out and grabbed his hair, pulling at it.

I'd never had sex like this before. it was like I'd been jettisoned into space and was spinning out of control at a thousand miles an hour. It was exhilarating and I was on the edge of my orgasm. It was building and I knew I was going to fall back to earth, hard. The crash was going to be epic.

"Nat, you feel so fucking good."

Surprising me, Freddie pulled out and flipped me over, grabbing my hips and lifted them so that my bum was in the air. He ran a hand over it.

"Perfect," he groaned as he pushed inside of me again. One hand on my hip, the other reached around and cupped my boob, massaging it as his thumb stroked my nipple.

Everything he did was setting my body on fire, while a host of emotions were balling up inside of me, building to an epic crescendo.

A slap landed on my bum, and it sent a spark to my clit as I edged a step closer to my orgasm. Freddie's hips went faster as he held on to both of mine.

"Nat, I'm so sorry. I'm going to come," he hissed.

"I want to touch myself."

"Do it," he growled.

As soon as my fingertips slicked through my wetness and touched my clit I shattered. It was like I'd detonated a bomb. I came hard and loud and as I did, Freddie came too. He was just as loud and hammered harder as the last vestiges of his orgasm flowed through him.

Breathing heavily, I tried to catch my breath, fighting to stay upright and not collapse on the mattress. Freddie's arm came around my waist and held me tight as he dropped kisses on my back between my shoulders.

"Fucking amazing," he finally said. "Totally fucking amazing."

He was right. It had been. I was powerful and feminine. Sexy and confident, and I wanted to do it all over again.

CHAPTER NINE

Something hard poked against my bum and I didn't hate it. It was a nice feeling, so I pushed back and wiggled. An arm came around my stomach and a deep growl sounded behind me.

"You're asking for trouble," Freddie said. "Keep pushing your arse against my dick and you'll regret it."

I turned to face him and was glad to see that he was smiling. Any worry I'd had that things would be awkward between us seemed to be unfounded. Freddie didn't look like he was embarrassed or thinking of ways to get rid of me.

"Morning." Too late I remembered that I hadn't brushed my teeth. It wasn't like I'd known I was going to have a sleep over and put a spare toothbrush in my bag. "Sorry, do I have dog breath?"

"Nope." Freddie yawned. "Sorry, but I had a late night."

"Did you?" I asked, with a grin. "Was it good?"

Lifting a finger to trace my profile, he shrugged. "It was okay. There was this hot girl in a sexy red dress who caught my eye."

I peered at him. "Really? I didn't realise you had a false eye."

Freddie groaned and buried his face in my neck. "That was terrible."

"I thought it was hilarious."

His hand moved to my bum, and he gave my bare cheek a squeeze, pulling me closer to him. His morning wood was now full mast and twitching against my stomach.

"Seriously, though," he said. "I had a great time last night."

My stomach swooped. I had totally been expecting him to give me excuses and reasons as to why I should go home. Why we should just put the night down to alcohol and raging hormones.

"Me, too." I took a deep breath. "But what about work?"

"What about it?" He started to trace a pattern on my back while watching me carefully.

"Well, what we did. Will it alter things at work?"

His hand trailed down my spine towards my bum and when his finger traced low, my eyes widened. Freddie grinned and dragged it up to my lower back.

"No, Nat, it won't alter things at work. Although, I may want to fuck you on my desk once in a while."

I blinked. "*Freddie.*"

"Well, I might. I've fantasised about it long enough."

"You have?"

"I told you, nine months, Natty," he replied. "Nine months I've been thinking about what underwear you might be wearing under those tight skirts."

"Wow, you really are a perv."

He pinched my bum and made me squeal. When he ran a soothing hand over it there was a flutter between my legs.

"The office will be fine," he said. "We'll make it work."

"What happens when the month is up?" Freddie frowned. "Will I have to order my own flowers?"

He pulled back, his hand stilled, and he frowned. "What does that mean?"

"Freddie, your limit is a month. I should know."

"That's different. They're different."

I wasn't stupid and nor was I clingy or needy. "It's fine, Freddie. I get it. You're my boss and it's sex at the end of the day."

Freddie wiggled his eyebrows. "It could be sex at the beginning of the day too, if you fancy it."

"Maybe, but can we finish our discussion first?" I tweaked his nipple, and when he laughed I marvelled at how easy things were between us. It was like we were months into a relationship. Which I supposed we were, it just happened to be employer and employee.

"Why do we need to discuss it?" Freddie asked. "Can't we just go with the flow?"

"I don't expect anything from you. If this is just one night that's fine, I just don't want things to be awkward at work."

Freddie frowned and cupped my face. "Do you want it to be just one night?"

How the hell did I answer that?

I'd be stupid to say yes. The sex was amazing. He was amazing and we got on brilliantly, and that was the worry. What if work became a problem? I could get another job, easily, I'd been headhunted a couple of times in the last year, but I liked working with Freddie which was why I'd stayed.

"I like you, Freddie," I started. "I like working for you. However, I also loved having sex with you. I'd like to do it again but if you don't want that, well, that's fine, too."

He smiled softly. "You are nothing like any other woman I've ever met."

"Hopefully, that's a good thing."

"Oh yeah, it definitely is." He moved closer and his impressive hard on pushed up against my stomach. "I want to have sex with you again, too. It was amazing and I think we can both handle it at work."

"Sex?"

He laughed with a deep chuckle. "Like I said, my desk has been a great fantasy of mine for months." Smoothing his hand up and down my back, I relaxed against him. It was a great place to be, in his arms, in his warm and comfy bed. "If it ever gets to a point where things are difficult then we'll work it out."

"You'll find me another job?"

The smile fell from his face and his body stiffened. "No. That will never happen. How the hell would I manage without you?"

"You'd find someone." I kissed him quickly. "Not as good as me, but there'd be someone out there. Harriet from accounts would be great."

"I'm not having fucking Harriet from accounts working for me," he protested. "Her breath smells of peanuts."

Giggling, I snuggled down under the duvet. He was right because she lived off them. I didn't think in the time I'd worked there that I'd ever seen her eat anything else. Not even a sandwich at lunchtime.

"We see how things go then?" Freddie asked.

"Yep. We see how things go."

"Excellent. Now," he said, leaning in, "how about that beginning of the day sex?"

CHAPTER TEN

With a little spring in my step, I carried the box of donuts to the cash register and joined the queue.

"Mid-morning snack?"

I turned to see an old man wearing a brown coat with something questionable down the front of it. His eyebrows were raised above the thick brown rims of his glasses, and he was nodding at the box in my hand.

"Sorry?"

"Mid-morning snack." He pointed a grubby finger. "For you."

I looked at the donuts before my gaze went back to him. "Well, not just for me."

"You sure now?" He tutted and shook his head.

"Maybe if you didn't partake, you might get rid of some of that." His finger then circled in the area of my stomach.

"I beg your pardon?" I blinked, wondering whether it was an offense to hit an OAP with a box of donuts.

"You'd maybe lose some weight if you cut those things out."

"Hey." The guy behind the old man, poked him in his shoulder. "You need to stop being so bloody rude."

The pensioner turned and looked him up and down. "Did you say something?"

"Yeah, I did." The man who was wearing a high-vis' jacket and trousers leaned closer to the old man. "I said there is no need to be so rude." He looked around him to me. "You take no notice of him, love. You're bloody gorgeous."

"She's overweight, that's what she is."

"Excuse me," I protested. "Not that it's any of your business but I happen to be very fit. I may be overweight as you put it, but at least I'm not rude and ignorant."

"Yeah, exactly," high-vis' guy said. "So, keep your damn rude opinions to yourself."

It was then my turn to pay, so I turned my back

on him, determined that I wouldn't cry. I didn't care what he thought but I was still humiliated. What gave someone the idea that it was okay to speak to people like that?

"Sorry, love," the cashier said. "He's a horrible old man. He upsets someone every time he comes in here."

I gave her a tight smile, warring between wanting to burst into tears or yelling in his face what a shit of a human being he was.

"Thanks," I replied and flashed my bank card at the reader. When it beeped I had never been more grateful to pick up my donuts.

"Hey, love."

I didn't want to have to look at the old man again, but high-vis' man obviously wanted to talk to me, and he'd been lovely. It would have been rude to ignore him. With a sigh, I turned and looked around the mean old buzzard.

"Yes?"

"If you ever fancy going for a drink one night..." He held up his mobile and waggled it. "Maybe I could take your number."

He couldn't be nice to me. It would make me cry.

"Thank you, but you don't have to."

He grinned. "I don't *have* to do anything. I want to."

"I'm kind of seeing someone."

"Hah." The old man scoffed, and I took a deep breath, determined not to look at him.

"That's a shame." High-vis' man shrugged.

"Thank you." When he gave me a gentle smile, I almost offered him my donuts. Instead, I gave him a wave and left, *with* the donuts.

By the time I got back to work I was fuming and almost stormed all the way back to the supermarket. The only reason I didn't was because I knew the old man would no longer be there. Otherwise, I'd have gone back and hit him over the head with my stiletto.

"What the hell is wrong with you?" Freddie asked as I slammed into his office. He pushed his chair back from the desk to study me.

"Some people are just twats."

"Right. And who would that person be, specifically?"

"Some old bloke who was at the supermarket. He fat shamed me." The hideousness of the situation hit me again and my chest constricted.

"He did fucking what?" Freddie pushed out his chair and rushed to me. He held the tops of my arms and stooped down to look in my eyes. "Who was it? Is it someone I know? Was it someone who works here, because I'll fire them."

I shook my head. "No. It wasn't anyone you know. I told you it was an old man at the supermarket."

Freddie's nostrils flared. "At the supermarket?" When I nodded, he pulled me to him and kissed my forehead.

Damn, he'd make someone a great boyfriend.

"And what did the old bastard say?" Freddie took my hand and led me back to his chair. He sat. "Come on." He patted his knee. "Sit down and tell me all about it."

I glanced at the door. "What if someone comes in?"

He arched a brow. "The door's closed. They know not to come in if it's closed."

That was true, *they* did.

"I'll be too heavy."

Freddie pulled me down. "Don't be so stupid. Tell me what was said."

I relayed the story of the old man and my donuts and the nice man in the high-vis' jacket.

"Fucking bastard," Freddie growled. "How dare he!"

"Things like that usually never upset me, but I wanted to cry."

He gazed at me for a few seconds, then put a hand to the back of my head and pulled me in for a kiss. It was soft and quick and accompanied with a heavy sigh.

"I'm sorry he upset you."

"I hate that he hit a nerve." I picked at the stitching of the centre seam down the front of my skirt. "It was horrible."

"What a piece of shit." Freddie's arms wrapped around me. "Good on the other guy for sticking up for you."

"The cashier said he upsets people all the time. When the other guy asked for my number he made this huffing sound."

Freddie stilled. "He did what?"

He didn't sound angry but there was a tension in his jaw and his nostrils were flared.

"He huffed."

"Not him, the other guy," he ground out.

"He asked for my number." I shook my head. "He was just being nice. Probably thought it would cheer me up."

"More like he was thinking about feeling you up." He cleared his throat. "And did you give him your number?"

"No. And, like I said, he was just being nice." I laughed. "He wasn't thinking about feeling me up."

"I think you'll find he was." Freddie's eyes narrowed. "Cheeky bugger." His bottom lip stuck out in a pout.

"What's wrong?"

"He asked for your bloody phone number. That's what's wrong."

Oh my god, he was jealous.

Finding it cute, I couldn't help but kiss him on the corner of his mouth. When I moved to pull away, Freddie's hand went to the back of my head and kept me there. His tongue probed until I allowed the kiss to deepen. My hands threaded through his hair, as his thumb whispered against my nipple over the top of my blouse and I arched towards him, brushing my boobs up against the hard planes of his chest. I needed more. Excitement surged through me as Freddie's hand moved up my skirt and a deep growl emanated from his throat when he reached my stocking top.

"How many fucking times have you worn these

in the office?" he asked, pushing a finger under the garter of my suspender belt. "Shit, Nat."

"Most days," I said breathily. "So much healthier than tights."

"I'm not sure they're good for my health. I might die of too much blood flowing to my dick." His lips went to my neck, and I shivered as his finger drew a circle on my thigh. "They're amazing. I think I need to see you wearing them and nothing else."

His voice was low and seductive and was as much to blame for the throbbing between my legs as his fingers were.

"I seriously want to fuck you right now."

I squirmed as the hardness in his trousers pushed against my bum. "I think I'd like that too," I whispered.

Extricating his hands from my underwear, Freddie tapped my thigh and pushed up from his chair.

"I need to lock the door."

"I thought that you said *they* wouldn't come in."

"Better to be sure seeing as I'm going to fuck you over my desk," he said against my ear. "I really don't want anyone seeing you naked, except for me."

I swallowed and stuttered out, "O-okay."

Freddie strode purposefully across the room and turned the key in the door. He then closed the blind at the glass panel in the wall by the door before going over to the window and doing the same. His office overlooked some woods at the back of the building. They were dense and overgrown, but you never knew when someone could be out there bird watching.

Steadying myself with a hand on his desk, I watched as Freddie stalked back to me. His gaze never left me as he took off his suit jacket and threw it onto the green velvet sofa. His attention then went to his shirt, undoing each button slowly. Too slowly.

"Bloody hell, Freddie. Hurry up, would you?"

He smirked and took a step closer. "Get undressed, Nat," he demanded.

I squirmed as the throb between my legs matched the rhythm of the butterflies swooping in my stomach. He looked like a much sexier James Bond than I'd ever seen in the films. In fact, I made a mental note to contact the producers and suggest they screen-test him.

Mirroring his movements, I undid the buttons of my blouse until my cerise pink bra was on display. It was a balcony bra, and once again my boobs looked spectacular in it. I let the red silk of my blouse drop from my shoulders and onto the floor and when Freddie inhaled sharply, I smiled.

The pale blue cotton of his shirt went the same way and my mouth watered at the sight of his body. Freddie's hands then went to the brown leather belt at his trousers and he unbuckled it. As it hung down, he unbuttoned his trousers then slowly unzipped them, giving me a glimpse of white boxer-briefs against his tanned stomach.

"Your turn."

I inhaled a ragged breath and felt around the back of my skirt for the zip. I unzipped it and with my hands at my hips, pushed the skirt down until it pooled around my red stilettos. The only sounds in the room were Freddie's heavy breathing and his trousers dropping softly to the floor. When he kicked off his shoes and reached down to take off his socks, he continued to watch me. His erection strained at his boxers, and I could see his beautiful, smooth crown peeking above the waistband.

"You look amazing," he said as he straightened. "In fact, I don't think I've ever seen anything so bloody beautiful."

Heat crept up my neck to my face, and I wondered if it had gone as pink as my underwear. Feeling confident, I widened my stance and placed my hands on my hips. Freddie clearly found me sexy, his hard-on proved that, but the way his eyes scored over my body and my face, and the softness of his smile made me feel special.

"I think you need to keep your shoes on. Those and the suspenders. Just lose the knickers, gorgeous."

My heart almost beat out of my chest as he moved towards me, stopping only when we were almost toe to toe. He'd called me gorgeous, and it infiltrated my soul. Confidence oozed from every single one of my pores because I knew I was driving him wild.

I reached for the waistband of my knickers and shimmied them past my hips and down my legs. Lifting my left leg out of them, they hung from my right shoe before I kicked them away. As the anticipation built and my breathing got heavier, my nipples ached for contact and my clit throbbed for attention.

Freddie pushed his boxer-briefs down and stepped out of them as he swallowed. "Lean over the desk, hands on the wood, and arse in the air."

His voice was low and masterful, and it sent an electrical shock straight between my legs. I was wet and desperate for him, so did as he commanded.

Hands to the wood and arse in the air.

Freddie moved behind me and smoothed a hand over my bum. He let his fingers trace the curve before going between my legs. When he slowly dragged them through my arousal, I gasped. When he pushed them inside of me, I cursed.

"Shit."

Desperate for him to touch my tiny bud of nerves, I pushed my hips back, hoping to get some kind of relief. With his fingers thrusting a rapid rhythm, Freddie nipped at my shoulder before kissing down to my spine, all the time finger fucking me with one hand while the other stroked reverently over my bum. The softness of his kisses, the silky touch of his hand, and the hard thrusting were all-encompassing. The whole of my body was being assaulted by him in the best possible way. He was everywhere but I wanted more.

"Freddie," I gasped as he flicked at my clit with his thumb. "God."

"You're so fucking wet."

His body lifted from mine, and I heard his drawer open before his wallet landed on the desk in front of me. "Condom, gorgeous. In my wallet."

I flipped it open and found two condoms in the notes section. Using my teeth, I ripped open the foil before pulling it out and passing it to Freddie. With a muttered thanks, he removed his fingers from me and took a step back. I looked over my shoulder and watched as he rolled the pink latex down his shaft. Making quick work of it, Freddie then raised his eyes to meet mine and grinned.

"Open your legs wider."

I did as he asked and turned back to look down at the desk, bracing myself for Freddie's powerful thrust. He didn't disappoint me as strong hips thrusted, and his dick entered me fast and hard. The desk shifted forward with the force and my eyes bulged as Freddie's dick hit the spot, making me cry out,

"Oh my god, Freddie."

"This fucking arse is amazing." He slapped a hand on my bare cheek and my pussy clenched. "Shit, so damn good."

As he pushed in and out, I pressed back and groaned out a needy moan. Freddie chuckled and took the strap of my bra, pulling it down. His fingers squeezed and kneaded my breast before pinching at my sensitive nipple. My skin was on fire, tingling all over where our bodies met. I clawed at the desk, screwing a piece of paper underneath my fingertips as the tight ball grew in the pit of my stomach. His lips sucked on my shoulder, and my hips followed his rhythm as we both chased our release. When Freddie pressed a flat palm against my spine, his other hand went to my clit and rubbed a circle around it. As he groaned out my name my legs began to tremble, and I swear I could feel Freddie's heartbeat against my back. As everything reached a crescendo, our movements sped up and we fell together.

Sated and exhausted, I sagged against the cool wood and Freddie braced himself over the top of me. His hands were on the desk, next to mine as we both tried to catch our breath.

"You know, that's probably the best meeting I've ever had." Freddie placed his hands on top of mine and entwined our fingers.

I looked at him over my shoulder and grinned. "I forgot to take notes."

"Aww shit, really?" I nodded and he shrugged. "We'll just have to do it again."

When Freddie moved his hips I knew he meant it. I was up for it and pushed back.

"You and your greedy little pussy," he whispered against my ear.

A slow rhythm started and as I reached behind me to put my hand to his neck someone started banging on the office door. Freddie paused mid-thrust and when I gasped, he slapped a hand over my mouth.

"Hello. Fred, are you in there, mate?"

"It's fucking Jacob," Freddie hissed close to my ear.

"What do we do?"

"Fred. Have you forgotten we've got that call with Luis Gonzales? He's on the line in five minutes. You'll need to dial in."

"Fuck, I forgot. Why didn't you remind me?" he whispered in my ear.

"Because I didn't know." I pushed my bum back. "Get off."

Freddie pulled out of me, and when I turned around he was standing there, semi-hard and still wearing a used condom.

"You never told me. How am I supposed to assist you if you don't tell me when you organise meetings over a bloody pint on a Friday night?"

"I didn't organise it at the pub." He threw his hands in the air. "I was sure I told you."

Grabbing my discarded knickers, I looked him up and down. Still naked, *still wearing a condom.* "Well, you didn't. Now get dressed. And sort something out with Jacob."

"Like what?"

"Freddie! I know you're in there because your car is outside, and Nova said you came back an hour ago."

"Sodding Nova," Freddie groaned.

Nova was our receptionist, and no one got in or out of the building without her seeing them and conducting an interrogation.

"If you're having a wank or something, this is not the time."

Giggling, I pulled on my knickers. "Not exactly a wank."

Freddie narrowed his gaze on me, but then looked at the door when Jacob tried the handle again. He looked down at his now flaccid penis and pulled off the condom.

"Grab your clothes and get under the desk."

"What?"

"Please, Nat. Get your clothes and get under the desk." I shook my head and started to snag up the rest of my clothes. "One minute, Jacob," he yelled towards the door as he looked around the room, the condom between his finger and thumb.

"What the fuck are you doing and where is Natty?"

"Don't know."

"What do you mean, you don't know?" Jacob

yelled through the door. "You always know where she is." Jacob laughed. "Even when she's not working."

Freddie's eyes went wide, and he shook his head. "I do not. I swear. Honestly, Nat, I'm not a stalker."

I rolled my eyes and got down on the floor and pushed under his desk. "Get dressed," I hissed. "And wrap it in a piece of paper before you put it in the bin."

"Good thinking." He snatched a piece from his desk and dropped the condom onto it and then screwed it all into a ball.

"Freddie! Open the damn door."

"Okay, okay," Freddie yelled impatiently and threw the evidence in the waste paper bin.

As I hid under his desk, I heard him dragging on his clothes in superfast time before opening the door of his office.

"What the hell were you doing?" Jacob asked as his voice came closer.

"I was having a kip."

"Really? And what's got you so tired?" Jacob sounded sceptical as his feet appeared only inches from me. I held my breath. "Have you been moving your desk?"

"No," Freddie answered as he flopped down into his chair and his knees almost hit me in the face.

"Oh," Jacob said, moving away from the desk. "I must be mistaken. It looks like this has moved at least a couple of feet."

"No. Nope. No. Not moved it." Freddie cleared his throat. "Right, are you going to go back to your office, and we can get this call up and running?"

Jacob didn't speak immediately, but after a few seconds of anxious silence, he said. "I think I'll stay here with you." I was sure I heard him chuckle. "It's much warmer than my office."

"But w-wouldn't you much rather go to your own office?" Freddie asked, tentatively.

"Nope."

The guest chair was pulled up close and the next thing I knew, Jacob's feet were under the desk and inches from me and I was trapped by two sets of knees in well-cut trousers.

"Is it me or does it smell in here?" he asked.

He was right. It did. Of sex. And it was growing cold, but then that would probably be because I was sitting huddled in just my underwear. I couldn't even try to put my clothes on because I didn't have much room to manoeuvre.

"Let's just go to your office," Freddie said. "I

need to speak to marketing anyway, so I can speak to them on the way."

"We don't have time," Jacob replied, sounding like he was distracted by something. "Just get logged on and do the call."

I was trapped and to make matters worse, I needed the loo. I needed my post-sex pee. It was not helping my chances of avoiding a water infection. I tugged on Freddie's trouser leg. Maybe he'd realise it was a sign for help.

His foot moved closer, and he nudged me with it. I reached my hand up his trouser leg and plucked at a hair.

"Oww!"

"What's wrong with you?" Jacob asked. "Why are you yelling?"

"Nope. Nothing. No reason." Freddie coughed and nudged me with his foot again.

He was just ignoring me! I was going to get bloody pneumonia or at least piles if he didn't do something quick. Not to mention a UTI.

"Okay," Jacob said with a sigh. "Let's get this meeting going."

"Right, I still think it'd be better in your office." Freddie sounded petulant.

"Yeah, well you would say that," Jacob replied.

"Why would I?"

"Because," he said with a laugh, "Natty could then get out from under the desk where she's been since I caught you having sex

I gasped, which morphed into a scream when Jacob's face appeared. He grinned and waved, then winked.

"Hi, Natty."

I buried my face in my hands and groaned, "Hi, Jacob."

"Fuck's sake," Freddie groaned, and I heard a thud, which I was sure was his head hitting the desk.

"Just one question?" Jacob asked, still grinning at me.

"What?" I muttered, *still* hiding my face.

"If you take us to court for sexual harassment, please make sure they know it was just Freddie who couldn't keep his dick in his pants."

Well, what a great day I'd had.

CHAPTER ELEVEN

Getting from under Freddie's desk had to be the single most embarrassing moment of my life. Jacob at least left the room, but he couldn't stop laughing. They'd eventually held the meeting and our day had continued as normal.

I was certainly ready for a large glass of wine with Andrew, who I was meeting in a bar close to the office. When I pushed open the double doors, the sight of my best friend with two large glasses of wine in front of him was the best thing ever.

"Am I glad to see you," I said as I picked up the glass of wine. I hadn't even sat down, that was how needed it was. "Hey, had a good day?"

Andrew raised his glass to mine. "Not bad. What about you?"

I gave a half shrug. "Ups and downs."

It had been more in and out for a while there.

"Do I want to know?"

"Maybe after we've eaten." I sighed and took another long sip of wine. "It's not a story I can tell on an empty stomach."

"Now I'm intrigued." Andrew pushed the menu at me. "I know what I'm having so pick quick. I need the gossip."

I didn't need to look at the menu. "Cheese and onion pie, chips and beans."

Andrew grinned and went to order our food, while I thought about what had happened on Freddie's desk.

"And Jacob didn't say anything else about it?" Andrew's eyebrows were almost in his hairline.

"He just laughed until he was almost pissing himself." I'd thought he was going to have a seizure at one point. "In all seriousness, though, I wonder if we should tell HR."

"Isn't that up to Freddie?"

"I suppose so. I think I'll mention it to him. What do you think?"

Andrew nodded. "Yep, mention it. I think you should, especially if it's going to be a regular thing."

"I hardly think twice is regular." I'd already told Andrew about the post auction sex. Freddie had dropped me home, so I couldn't deny anything to Andrew, seeing as I was wearing a pair of my boss's sweatpants and one of his t-shirts at the time.

"That's a relationship for Freddie, isn't it? And you've got at least three weeks and four days left to enjoy it."

That made me bristle a little, but it was my own fault. I was the one who'd told Andrew all about Freddie's girlfriends and their one-month shelf life.

"I am worried about how it'll affect work," I sighed.

"Clearly it's going to make it more exciting." Andrew laughed. "A shag every afternoon on the boss's desk is bound to make the days go quicker."

"Oh, stop it." I pushed my empty plate away. "Do you want pudding?"

Andrew shook his head. "You?"

I looked at the menu and considered the options. They did a lovely chocolate brownie trifle. "Want to share?"

"No thanks."

I pushed the menu away from me. "I couldn't eat a whole one, so no."

Andrew narrowed his eyes on me. "You're not in love, are you?"

"What?"

"In love? Are you in love with Freddie?"

"What the hell gave you that idea?"

He pointed at the menu. "You don't want pudding."

"I'm full."

"Well, you certainly were when you were pushed over Freddie's desk, that's for sure."

"*Andrew.*"

We both started to laugh, and I poured us both another large glass of wine. "Tell me about Miles. How's that going?"

He pointed a finger at me. "Deflecting, Natalie."

"I'm not," I protested.

"Liar. However, I'll let you off seeing as I want to talk about him." He gave a contented sigh and smiled at me, looking all sated and dreamy. "I really like him, Natty."

"I can tell. If you're not with him, you're on the phone *to* him."

"He makes me feel incredible." Andrew's cheeks pinked. "I think he might be the one."

I sighed inwardly. Andrew was kind of like the women in Freddie's life, ergo he usually got dumped after a month or so. Each time he was convinced he'd found the one.

"I know what you're thinking," Andrew added.

"Sweetheart." I grabbed his hand and gave it a squeeze. "I just worry about you, that's all."

"He's different, Natty. I swear."

"That's brilliant. He does seem nice." And he did.

Andrew smirked and leaned closer. "Do you think Freddie might be the one?"

I waved him anyway. "Don't be so stupid. It's just sex."

"Really? There isn't a little bit of you that wants something more, is there? I mean, he's pretty hot and rich as fuck."

"That doesn't make someone the perfect partner," I argued. "Don't get me wrong, it all helps but I wouldn't marry someone just for their money."

"What if they had a big cock too?"

I wiggled an eyebrow. "Goes without saying." As I laughed, Andrew stared at me with a grin on his face. "What's wrong with you?" I instinctively wiped at my face. "Do I have a bogie?"

He shook his head. "Nope, but you might want to freshen your lipstick up."

"Why?"

He nodded over my shoulder. "Because Freddie just walked in."

My heart started to thud before dropping to my stomach, doing a somersault before shooting up to my throat. Excitement and fear combined at the idea that my lover, *my sexy boss,* had walked through the door.

"Who is he with?" I hissed. "On his own? With a woman?"

"A tall, dark-haired guy."

I took a swig of wine. "Does the other guy look like a tall James Marsden?"

"Is James Marsden short?" Andrew asked.

I shrugged. "Well, I've never seen him in the flesh, but he doesn't appear to be tall. So, does the other guy look like James Marsden?"

Andrew leaned to one side and craned his neck. "Erm, yep there's a resemblance. Freddie looks like the Fifty Shades guy, doesn't he? I've never noticed before."

"Really? You think so?" I glanced over my shoulder and caught sight of Freddie at the bar. He was leaning over it and talking to the barman while

Jacob looked down at his phone. I turned back to Andrew. "I always thought he looked like the guy from the aftershave ad."

"Much more Christian Grey. Anyway, he's here."

I rolled my eyes. "So, I see, and that's Jacob with him."

"Oh okay." Andrew took another look. "Must be nice working for two hotties. My bloody boss looks like Phil Mitchell in a curly wig."

"What's he doing?" I asked.

"Passing a pint to the other guy. And now they're moving away from the bar, and they're looking for a table and... hey, Freddie, hiya." He started to waving and grinning inanely.

"What the hell are you doing?" I hissed. My skin prickled and a heat swept over me as I reached for Andrew's glass of wine and knocked it back. "Is he coming over."

Before he could answer, two bodies appeared in my periphery and my stomach swooped again.

I looked up and smiled. "Hey."

Earlier that day, I'd had my arse in the air while he drilled me from behind. He'd seen me naked. He'd kissed me like I was his personal buffet. He'd given me three orgasms in total. Yet I was shy and embarrassed about seeing him in the pub.

"Hey, Nat." His warm smile made me feel even more giddy.

"Join us," Andrew said. "Nice to see you again by the way."

Freddie turned to Andrew and nodded. "Yeah, you, too." He then looked at Jacob, who was grinning at me like a fool. "Did you want to—?"

"Oh, yep, sure," Jacob said, pulling out a chair. "Let's sit." He held out his hand to Andrew. "Jacob."

"Andrew."

They shook hands while Freddie moved his chair a little closer to mine. "You okay?" he asked, nudging me with his shoulder. "After earlier."

My skin heated up at the memory. Funny, though, it was remembering the sex which had me hot and bothered, Jacob catching us at it not so much.

"I'm fine, but did Jacob say anything about seeing me in my undies?"

"Nope." He raised an eyebrow. "It wasn't exactly a bad view for him, though."

"I'm just glad that I was wearing matching knickers and bra."

"I think I'd have preferred if you were wearing a

sack." He glanced over at Jacob who was talking animatedly to Andrew.

"He only has eyes for Rebecca, I doubt he barely noticed."

"Yet you're glad you were wearing matching knickers and bra."

I grinned at him. "Of course. Any self-respecting woman would be." When his arm went around the back of my chair, a warmth swept over me. His bicep leaning against my shoulder made me feel safe and protected. Yet, like I'd told Andrew, I was aware we could be treading a close line to unprofessionalism. It worried me that we might just be the HR department's biggest nightmare. I leaned closer to Freddie. "Do you think maybe we should let HR know what's going on between us?" When he didn't speak, I wondered if I'd misunderstood everything. "I mean you may not feel it's necessary. You know if, well... if... I don't know..."

Freddie frowned. "Why would we need to tell them? I'm the boss."

"For that very reason, Freddie," I whispered. "It's protection for you."

"What the hell do I need protecting from?" He paused his pint glass at his lips. "Are you going to murder me while I'm shagging you or something?"

I gasped. "No. What an awful thing to say."

He chuckled and pulled gently at my hair. "Don't Black Widow spiders do that?"

"Yes. After they've been shagged, as you so eloquently put it."

"Obviously." He scoffed. "Get your orgasm first and then kill the selfish bastard who gave it to you."

"Typical behaviour of a woman, because you know we're all venomous deep down."

Freddie's lip twitched as he appeared to try and hide his smile. "Evil little shits."

We both burst out laughing, earning the attention of Jacob and Andrew.

"What's so funny?" Jacob asked.

"Nothing," Freddie replied. "Just Nat deciding how she's going to murder me."

"Oh, I've thought about that many, many times." Without any trace of humour, Jacob shook his head. "He's a nightmare."

"I am not. I'm a great boss, aren't I, Nat?"

"When you're giving her orgasms," Andrew muttered loud enough for us all to hear.

Jacob spat beer across the table, while I stretched to kick Andrew in the shin. Freddie just grinned, seemingly unaffected by the comment.

"Sorry," Andrew groaned, as he leaned down to rub his leg. "Did I say that a bit too loud?"

"Just a bit." I looked at Freddie, worried that it may have finally sunk in what Andrew had said. "I'm sorry, Freddie. I don't want you to think we've been gossiping, but he's my friend and—"

"Hey," he said, holding up his hand. "It's fine. Just one thing."

"What?" I asked.

"Will the quality of the orgasms affect your feedback on *Rate Your Boss*?"

CHAPTER TWELVE

The candles on the tables were the only lighting in the restaurant which was in a basement. The walls were bare brick, yet everything was warm, cosy and romantic. Plus, we were twenty miles out of the city so unlikely to bump into anyone we worked with. It was me who'd insisted on it, seeing as Freddie had wanted to go to a lovely restaurant close to the office, because in his words, 'who gives a shit if anyone sees us?'.

"How's your steak?" he asked, reaching for his wine and taking a sip.

"Amazing." I closed my eyes and moaned as my taste buds practically sparkled. "What about your lobster?"

"Also amazing." Freddie's eyes twinkled as he smiled. "You want more wine, gorgeous?"

He moved to pick up the bottle in the ice bucket, but before he had chance, the waiter was at the table in a flash. He had to be a vampire with that speed.

"It's fine," Freddie told him, waving him away. "I'll pour."

"Are you sure, sir?"

"Absolutely." We watched the waiter back away before Freddie poured me another glass of wine.

"I hate being waited on like that," Freddie said as he tucked back into his meal.

"That's what happens when you have money."

"Yeah, and I hate that part. I've worked as a waiter to make money and it's fucking hard work. They don't need to be hanging around doing stuff for me that I'm perfectly capable of doing myself because I have hands."

"He's just trying to get a decent tip." I put another piece of meat in my mouth and closed my eyes against the taste sensation.

When I opened them, Freddie was staring at me with a dirty smirk that promised a whole host of things.

"What?" I asked, placing my knife and fork down.

"You. Making those noises." He leaned over the table and whispered, "You're fucking turning me on, Nat."

I winked at him and licked my lips, knowing it would make him even hornier. I loved playing with him. Who would have known that big boss Freddie who ran a multi-million-pound company could be so easy to toy with?

"You know, I may have to fuck you senseless later."

I raised a brow. "I'm hoping so."

"Do you think we could get this to take away?" he asked with a wiggle of his eyebrows. "I can get the car to come for us now."

I'd offered to drive us in Andrew's car, but Freddie wouldn't hear of it. He'd wanted us both to relax after a long week at work, so had hired a driver. It had felt a bit over the top, but I guessed when the guy you were seeing was a millionaire, it was probably the norm. I was more used to dates who expected you to pay half towards the petrol.

"As much as I'd like to say yes, I would like to stay and finish dinner." I shifted my chair closer to the table and leaned into Freddie's space. "I promise that I'll make it up to you later, though."

Freddie stretched across and dropped a quick

kiss to my lips, his fingers lingering on my cheek as he pulled back slowly. My pulse sky rocketed at his touch, and I second guessed my request to stay at the restaurant. His eyes looked deep into mine and were full of promise and inuendo. Things had changed a lot between us, very quickly, and I wasn't sure whether it was the right thing or not. I'd always liked him, we'd always worked well together, but now we were so much more after one night at an auction. The worry work and how it could affect it kept nagging at me, though. It was constantly in my head and kept me awake at night.

"Can I ask you something?"

Freddie looked quizzically at me. "You look serious."

"No. I'm not, I'm just concerned."

"About?" He leaned back with his glass held against his chest, his eyes watching me carefully.

"Work, and don't roll your eyes at me, Freddie." I grinned at him because he looked like a cute toddler. "You know I'm apprehensive about it."

"Nothing will change regarding work. I've told you this, Nat." He took a sip of his wine before continuing. "I know you're anxious, but I promise you we've got this. And Jacob won't say a word."

I blushed as the mere mention of Jacob almost

catching us. "I know, but I still think you need to let HR know."

"Why? It's my company."

"Exactly. I don't want anyone thinking I'm with you for that reason or that you've coerced me into something *because* you're my boss."

"I'll have something to say to anyone that does. In fact," he said, tapping a finger on the table, "I'll sack them."

I laughed and reached for my wine. "And that is exactly what I'm talking about. That and what happens if this doesn't work out? We need to get advice on how we handle things, Freddie. You know we do."

He inhaled and I waited in the silence as he contemplated what I'd said. Finally, he nodded and put his glass down.

"Okay, I'll organise a meeting with HR. I'm only doing it for you, though." He reached across the table and gave my hand a squeeze. "But please stop worrying. It'll be fine, I promise you."

"Will you arrange the meeting or should I?" I asked with a smirk.

"You, obviously. You're the PA and I don't want to have to speak to people unless I absolutely have to." There was a glint in his eye as he reached for his knife and fork. "But beware, Nat, if she makes me hold a team meeting to announce our relationship status, I'll make you pay."

"And how will you make me pay?"

"That, gorgeous, would involve you being naked."

I giggled at how great that could be. "I think I changed my mind about taking the rest to go."

"Waiter!"

"Oh my... shit... Nat."

Freddie reached back and caught hold of the thick wooden slats of his head board, his knuckles turning white as he held on tight. I moved my mouth up and down his shaft, my tongue circling him each time I reached the tip.

Hissing through his teeth, Freddie's hand moved to grab my hair as his need for me increased. I moaned as he lifted his hips and pushed himself further into my mouth and I savoured the taste of him. Each moan from him increased my desire and I knew I was already on the brink of coming again... after already having one orgasm from Freddie's mouth.

When his hips began to thrust faster, I pumped him with one hand while my other cupped his balls. His legs stiffened and his toes curled, and when he let out a roar the result of his orgasm hit my tongue and I swallowed it down.

"Nat." The grip on my hair tightened and I relished the sting of it. "Fucking hell."

While Freddie continued to come, my hand went to my clit and I got myself to the same place. Falling over the edge with him.

As the tremors waved through us, our chests heaved with the exertion as sweat dripped down our bodies. My head dropped to his chest and I sighed.

"Wow."

"Too fucking right," Freddie replied, lacing his fingers with mine and resting them on his stomach. "But I'm not telling HR about it."

"Okay, I'll agree to keeping that part to us. Especially the thing you do with your tongue. I really don't want anyone knowing about that." I felt the rumble in his chest as he began to chuckle.

"Absolutely. That is," he said, kissing the top of my head, "for you only."

"Good to know."

He started to rub circles on my back with his

fingers and I sagged in relaxation, my bones feeling like jelly.

"I really don't want you to worry, Nat. Everything will be okay, I promise."

"I know." I sighed as his hand went closer to my bum. "I just..."

"What?" he asked after a few seconds of my words floundering into nothing.

How did I explain to him that I was feeling things that I probably shouldn't? That it was too easy to feel that way and way too early.

"Nothing," I finally replied. "I'm just being stupid."

Freddie rolled me to my back and pinned me beneath him. As he looked down at me with sincerity in his eyes, my chest swelled.

"There is nothing stupid about you, Nat. Not one single thing."

Then he kissed me, and I fell a little bit more.

CHAPTER THIRTEEN

It was like being in the headmistress' office. Exactly like the time I stuffed a yoghurt down Anthony Pearson's trousers. He was a dick who thought it was funny to flash all the girls every time we wore our gym skirts. He didn't even have a decent sized penis. Not that I'd know a decent sized one if it hit me in the face seeing as we were only fifteen.

Anyway, the top and bottom of it was, we were in our Head of HR's office. I was in one chair and Freddie in another. While I was sitting upright and rubbing my sweaty palms together, Freddie was lounging. He had one ankle resting on the opposite knee and had his fingers steepled under his chin, looking decidedly bored.

"And this relationship is consensual?" Melanie

asked, reaching forward to scribble something down on her pad.

"Well yeah," Freddie said. "I mean she's pretty domineering, but she always makes me say yes before she pulls my trousers down."

I rolled my eyes and gave Melanie a tight smile. "Yes, it's completely consensual."

"Good. And how long has it been going on?"

"Three weeks and four days," Freddie announced. "But I've fancied her for about nine months."

I still can't believe he's fancied me for nine months.

And God, was it only three weeks we'd been together?

The last three weeks had flown by with dinner dates, a weekend at the Lakes, a handful of overnight stays at Freddie's apartment. And, of course, lots and lots of sex.

Melanie's brows rose. "And did you pursue Natalie at any point during those nine months?"

"Stupidly, no." Freddie sighed heavily. "Listen, Mel, I only came to you today because Nat thought we should, and she's not shut up about it for the last three weeks. You see, she wants to be sure that I'm protected, because she's a good person." He smiled at me before turning back to Melanie. "I also want her protected, so," he leaned forward and circled his finger around Melanie's pad, "write up whatever it is you need to get us to sign and we'll sign it."

"There isn't anything that says you can't be in a relationship. It's your company, Freddie, and you've never asked for that to be a clause in anyone's contract. Therefore, if you want protection then we can either write something up or you could see your own solicitor."

Freddie groaned. "Mel, we've just started seeing each other, I haven't asked her to marry me."

That made my stomach go a little bit funny and it shouldn't have.

"Am I going to get fired if I keep on seeing Nat or not?"

Mel frowned. "It's, erm, your company, Freddie. You don't have a board or investors, so you're the only person who would have the authority to fire you."

Freddie gave a loud clap. "Excellent. Put it on record that everything is consensual, add a note to wherever you have to add a note and we're good to go." He stood up. "Right, Nat, let's go. I've got some emails I need you to send."

He was out of the door before I even had chance

to stand. Melanie sat open mouthed as she watched him leave.

"I'm sorry, Melanie. I don't think he thinks it's necessary."

"Clearly." She pulled her chair closer to her desk. "I'll get something written up which you can both sign."

"Thank you."

I had an urge to bow to her as I backed out of the room, she looked so regal sitting in her high-backed office chair with a grim face. Freddie was nowhere to be seen but everyone in the main office was staring at me. They evidently thought something was going on. I could see it on their gawping faces.

"Hey, Natty." Michael jumped up out of his seat, still wearing his headset. "Is everything okay?"

"Fine thanks, Michael."

I tried to continue walking but he grabbed hold of my arm. As he stretched to catch me, his headset was pulled off his head and catapulted back and hit him in the face. He then fell forward and stumbled, kicking the wastepaper basket and sending his stapler flying as he grabbed at it to try and save himself, only to crash into the corner of his desk.

"Are you okay?" I gasped as he bent over rub his knee. "Oh god, Michael."

"I'm fine," he gritted out. "All good."

I stooped down so that I could look him in the eye. "Do you want me to get the first aid kit?"

He shook his head and moaned. "No, I'm fine." He looked up and gave me a tight smile. "I wanted to check you were okay."

We both straightened, and when I looked around, I could see everyone was watching us.

"I'm fine, thank you, Michael." I winced. "I am worried about you though."

"No need. No need." He looked over to Melanie's office. "It's just you went in there with Freddie. You're not in trouble, are you? Because if you are, I can vouch for you."

"God, no," I laughed. "Everything is fine."

He frowned. "So, what did you go in there for? Are we all going to be made redundant?"

"No? Why on earth would you think that?"

"You were in HR *with* Freddie."

"But it wasn't because anyone is being made redundant. It was because..." I trailed off because I didn't want to tell him why I'd been in HR with Freddie.

"Will we get a pay off?" A voice came from right behind me.

I turned and almost banged my nose into that of

Rose from accounts. She was peering at me through the thick lenses of her glasses. They looked like she'd bought them for a 70's themed fancy dress party and then decided she quite liked them and not wearing them would be a waste of two pounds fifty.

"Rose, you're all mistaken. There's no redundancy."

"Natty, you know *he* should tell us if there's going to be redundancies," she said with a shake of her head, sounding thoroughly disgruntled. "We've all got bills and mortgages to pay."

"There's not going to be anyone losing their job, Rose!"

"You can tell us," Michael added, squeezing my forearm.

Frustrated, I pulled it away and turned to Rose. "You work in accounts. Don't you think you'd know if there was a problem?"

"Jacob doesn't tell me anything," she complained, crossing her arms over her ample chest.

"But you look at the figures every single day," I replied, pinching the bridge of my nose. "You would see. You'd notice."

"Not if Freddie and Jacob were hiding things from us. They might be cooking the books."

"*Cooking the books*? They wouldn't do that. You know they wouldn't do that,"

She shrugged with a disbelieving look on her face. "You say that but as Freddie's PA you'll have been told to keep it from us."

"But I haven't!"

"Again, you say that," Rose replied with a huff of breath.

"What the hell is going on?"

We all turned to see Freddie stalking towards us. His tie was loose, and his shirt sleeves were rolled up to show his lovely forearms, all tanned and sinewy and making me think about them being wrapped around me.

"Are we being made redundant?" Rose asked straight off the bat.

He stopped, putting his hands to his hips and furrowed his brow. "Whatever gave you that idea?"

"You did," she replied.

"I did? How the hell did I give you that idea?"

Michael raised a hand, like we were back in school. "Excuse me, Freddie, the fact that you went in to see Melanie with Natty is what gave us the idea."

"But it wasn't about redundancies." Freddie

looked thoroughly pissed off as he looked between Michael and Rose.

"So, what was it about?" Rose asked. "Hmm? Go on, tell us."

"Rose—"

"No, Natty," she interrupted me. "We need to know. Adrian and I have booked a holiday pot holing in Cumbria."

Freddie and I looked at each other and frowned. Rose's husband, Adrian, was around twenty-five stone and permanently used crutches.

"Adrian will be most upset if he can't go."

"Did you say pot holing?" Freddie asked.

"Yes," she snapped.

"Like those narrow pot holes that go down for miles?"

"Yes, Freddie. What don't you understand about it?"

Freddie shook his head. "Nope. No. Nothing. I get it, you and Adrian are going pot holing."

"Well, only if you don't sack us."

"I'm not bloody sacking you."

"Who's being sacked?" Penny from marketing appeared beside us. "Please don't say us. I've just booked a boob job."

"There you go," Rose said, pointing at Freddie.

"Not only are you spoiling my holiday but Penny's bosom as well."

"I'm not spoiling Penny's bosom," he yelled. "No one is getting sacked."

"So why did you go to HR with Natty?"

When I looked at him, I could see by his face that something was about to happen.

"Freddie," I hissed, and he grimaced.

"Come on, Freddie. Tell us," Michael insisted.

"Yes, Freddie," Rose added. "Tell us."

"Do I need to cancel my titty op?"

When I looked at him and saw his face was bright red, I knew it was too late.

"Because we're shagging, okay! That's why we were seeing Mel, alright?" He threw his hands in the air. "Because we're bloody shagging."

When he turned and stormed away, the only sound you could hear was Rose's false teeth as they dropped to the floor.

CHAPTER FOURTEEN

F reddie asked me to go out and get him some
lunch after our run in with the staff. The
reason being he didn't want to come out of his office
and face any of them. Rose's teeth falling out scared
him, worried they might chase across the carpet after
him. Because of that, he'd put his Do Not Disturb
on, thrusted a twenty pound note at me, and
requested comfort food and 'don't spare the fucking
calories'.

As I queued up to order his mac and cheese and
large chocolate brownie, I looked up at the special's
board. I was going to eat my lunch there rather than
risk the break room and more questions about my
relationship with Freddie.

"Is it true?" I heard behind me.

Twisting around, I was shocked to see Bethany standing there. Her face red and looking like she was about to blow steam from her nostrils. When I noticed a French stick in her hand, I literally blanched.

"Hi, Bethany." I forced a smile because I had a good idea what she was mad about. I pointed to the queue in front of me. "I'm just going to get lunch, could you just give me a couple of minutes?"

"I don't need a couple of minutes," she snapped. "I just want to know, Natty. Are you seeing Freddie?" Her voice suddenly got louder, and I sensed the rest of the café were watching us.

I looked over at the counter and could see there was only one portion of lasagne left in the chiller. If I moved out of the queue to deal with Bethany, I could lose my lunch. It was a moment of pure jeopardy.

Lasagne or Bethany?

When she stamped her foot, Bethany won. "Can we just go over here?" I asked, pointing to an alcove. "Maybe away from everyone." I didn't give her a choice and moved away, hoping she was following. When I turned around, thankfully she'd decided to join me.

"Okay," I said with a sigh, "what is it you want to know?"

"Are you seeing Freddie? Are you sleeping with my boyfriend?"

I scratched my forehead, considering how to answer her. "Actually, he's not your boyfriend. He ended things with you, remember?" The way she looked at me with her mouth open, I wasn't sure she did. "As for my relationship with Freddie, that isn't really any of your concern."

She lifted the French stick and I took a step back, my shoulders sagging in relief when she immediately lowered it again.

"It is my concern, because he's *mine*," she screamed, startling an old man who was eating soup.

I put a hand on her arm, hoping to calm her down, but it just made her eyes bulge out of her head. She was practically a googly-eyed emoji breathing fire.

"Bethany, please." I looked over at the man who was wiping soup from the front of his shirt and mouthed a sorry.

"No, Natty, you can't just get me to shut up about this. You've stolen him from me." She poked me in the shoulder with the bread. "I bet you were the reason he ended things with me, weren't you?"

"So, you agree that you're not together any longer?"

She threw her hands in the air, clutching the loaf like it was a light sabre. "Stop confusing me. You talking is getting me mixed up. He's mine. He's still mine."

I was getting frustrated and the queue for food was getting longer. If I missed the last piece of lasagne I was going to be pissed off. Bethany was no competition for pasta, minced beef and cheese, even if she did have a weapon.

"Right, please listen when I say this." I took a deep breath. "Freddie can do what he likes. It's his life and you are not his girlfriend. As for whatever is going on between me and him, that's not your business."

She opened her mouth to protest, but when I snapped my two fingers and my thumb together along with hissing a shush, she did it.

Note to one self, when dealing with Bethany treat her like a toddler who needs a nap. In that moment I totally understood why Freddie had dumped her and believe me I was usually Team Girlfriend.

"I just want to get my lunch, Bethany, so please leave me alone."

"I know you're lying, Natty. Someone told me."

Yes, and I could guess who that was. Bloody Penny seeing as she was 'gym buddies' with Bethany.

"Well, Penny shouldn't be discussing things that are talked about in the office outside of the office." I pinched the bridge of my nose. "If that's all, I'm going to get my lunch." Half my lunch break had gone, so I'd have to eat it back at the office, which pissed me off even more.

"Of course, you are," Bethany snapped as I moved to go past her. "Just go and eat as usual."

Ignoring her barbed comment, I breathed in my anger through my nose and told myself that there was a nice person in there somewhere.

"I have no idea what he sees in you anyway. I mean you're—"

I spun around and pointed a finger at her. "Don't even finish that sentence, Bethany, because if you do I will kick you in the shin."

"Oh my god! Are you threatening me? You are, aren't you? I'm going to sue you for this?" She yelled, jabbing her bread in my direction.

"Will you bloody shut up."

We both turned to see the old man with the soup looking up at us. His spoon was halfway to his mouth, and he was pointing a finger at Bethany.

"I'm so sorry," I apologised.

"It's not you, love, it's her," he grumbled, pointing his finger. "You're a spoiled little madam.

And if she says her fella isn't your fella any more then bloody believe her. Now," he said on a huge sigh, "can I finish my damn dinner?"

"Thank you," I mouthed to him silently. "Now, I'm going to get my lunch. Goodbye, Bethany."

There were two things I was going to give thanks for, the old man with the soup and the fact that there was one piece of lasagne left.

"You okay?" Freddie asked as I handed him his warmed up mac and cheese.

"Apart from having a run in with Bethany," I replied. "I'm great."

Freddie's face fell. "Oh fuck, what did she do?"

I retold my lunchtime tale, and about the old guy with the soup and Freddie sank further and further down in his seat.

"She's such an embarrassment," he groaned and reached for my hand, pulling me closer to him. "I'm so sorry, gorgeous."

I wrinkled my nose. "What did you see in her in the first place? She's a meany."

"I know. In my defence she never really showed that side of herself to me."

"Clearly she was on her best behaviour."

"I just sorry she laid into to you like that."

I chewed on the corner of my lip, wanting to get something off my chest. "Am I going to get this with every ex of yours, if I happen to bump into them while getting your lunch?"

He shook his head. "I swear, I generally have good taste."

I grinned. "Really? Is that right?"

He pulled me onto his lap and kissed me softly on the temple. "You bet it's right," he whispered against my ear. "Look at you."

Oh shit, I think I wanted this man even more than the lasagne waiting on my desk.

CHAPTER FIFTEEN

Freddie was pacing up and down his office while barking into his phone. The door was closed, yet I could still hear every word. He was a great boss but mess up and you knew about it. Currently he was letting his temper loose on the guy who ran a franchise in Yorkshire. We'd had a bunch of complaints about the place, from broken machinery, no clean towels, and even vermin in the changing room. Freddie was furious and after sending his Customer Service Manager, Bella, to check it out, his anger had gone to nuclear level.

"He on to Jason Vale?"

I looked up to see Jacob perching on the edge of my desk. He was dressed in a suit as usual, but as usual for him and Freddie, he'd lost his jacket and his tie was loosened.

"He's not happy at all."

"So, I can hear." Jacob winced. "To be fair, the stupid twat deserves it. Did you see the pictures that Bella took?"

"I did. They were awful. I'm surprised environmental health haven't closed it down." I looked at the clock on my computer and sighed. "He has a meeting in ten minutes. Nova said they've already arrived."

Jacob shrugged. "I guess you'll just have to leave them with Nova for the time being. Once he's in full flight there's no stopping him." He snagged a couple of mints from the glass bowl on my desk and threw them both into his mouth at the same time. "Anyway, I just wanted to let you know I'm off now. Rebecca has a check-up to determine whether she's going to need a c-section or not."

"Really? Why's that?"

"The awkward little devil is breech and is refusing to turn. He's only got a few days to sort his shit out."

I smiled because I knew how excited he and his wife were about the arrival of their first baby. "Let's hope he does."

He shrugged. "If he doesn't, at least Rebecca will be under the best care." He glanced towards Freddie's office. "Thanks to Fred."

I frowned. "Freddie?"

"Yeah, he's paying for her to go into a private maternity home."

My heart stuttered. I knew that Freddie was rich, but it was still a lovely thing to do for his friend and his wife.

"Wow."

Jacob chuckled. "Christ, Natty, look at the love hearts in your eyes."

"There are not."

There really were, I was sure of it. Things were getting better and better between us. The only problem was that we were three weeks and six days in and fast approaching the month mark.

"I think you're lying," he replied, tapping his hands down on the desk. "Just let him know that I've gone, and I'll see him tomorrow."

"Okay, and good luck with this afternoon."

He smiled and pushed up from the desk, leaving me alone listening to Freddie's rant for another ten minutes. When he finally stormed out of his office, his face was red with rage.

"What an absolute dick," he yelled.

I glanced towards the main office, knowing they were about to hear the string of curses that would no doubt continue for the next few minutes.

"The absolute cock." He threw his hands in the air. "He had excuse after excuse as to why he's ruining my fucking reputation. None of it his fault. Apparently," he said, banging his hand on my desk, "it's my fault because I bought cheap equipment and an old building. He has no fucking idea, none whatsoever. What an absolute prick." He stalked back to his office leaving the door open.

With a sigh, I stood up and followed him. "How did you leave it?"

"I've given him a week to sort it. I've told him if he doesn't then he's out and fuck any fees he's already paid for this year, he loses the lot. Get his contract out for me because I'm telling you, Nat," he turned to point at me, "I'm putting his price up."

"Can we do that? Do I need to call legal?"

He blinked slowly. "What?"

"Do you want me to call legal?"

"No. Why would I want you to do that?"

"To check we can change the conditions of his contract, especially if he's not out of it yet."

"If I say we're changing his contract then we're

changing it. I don't give a fuck what legal say. You're my PA not my business partner, so do as I ask."

I took a half step back and widened my gaze on him. "Sorry?"

"I think you heard. Now, get me the damn contract."

Like I said, when he lost it, he really lost it, and it appeared that it was my turn to suffer his wrath.

"Right, okay, will do." I started to leave his office but paused when I got to the door. "Oh, and your eleven o'clock is here."

He didn't respond so I went back to my desk to get on with doing my job and let Freddie simmer in his own juices.

The rest of my day had been quiet. Freddie took his clients out to lunch followed by another meeting at one of his gyms straight after. Things had been frosty before he'd gone. I'd been my usual professional self, but he was still in a mood and giving me one-word answers.

The guy may have been hot and gave amazing orgasms, but he was a big baby. Sulking like I'd taken his favourite toy from him. Well, he could sulk all he liked, I'd do my job and be professional, but I wouldn't suck up to him, just because he *was* hot and gave *amazing* orgasms.

When the door opened from the main office, Michael walked in carrying an iPad box. He was grinning as he approached my desk.

"Good afternoon."

"Hey, Michael. What can I do for you?"

"It's what I can do for you?" He placed the box in front of me and tapped it. "Your new iPad."

"I wasn't aware that I had an old one which needed replacing."

"Freddie says that everyone is to get one, but you had to have yours first." His expression changed and his lips turned down. "I guess it's because you're his girlfriend."

"First, I'm not his girlfriend and second, if I was that wouldn't be the reason for me having the first iPad. I'm probably getting the first one because I organise everything for Freddie." I stood up and held out my hand, but Michael kept hold of the box.

He looked contrite as he opened it. "Yes. I'm sorry. You're right. It's all set up for you. The password is here." He passed me a piece of paper. "Change it as soon as you can."

I took the piece of paper and placed it on my desk as Michael tapped at the screen. Silence fell, punctuated with heavy sighs from him as he did whatever it was he needed to do to the iPad. I could sense he wanted to say something but was holding back.

"Are you okay, Michael?"

He looked up at me, opened his mouth then closed it again. He took a breath, blew it out, then opened his mouth again.

"Spit it out."

I was expecting him to speak but instead he pounced at me, slapping his mouth against mine. He took my breath as he squeezed me tight and made a strange groaning noise from the back of his throat. My arms were pinned to my sides and my hands flapped like penguin's flippers as I tried to get free of him.

"I love you," he moaned, and his hand went to my bum.

"*Michael!*" I took advantage of his loosening his grip and managed to get two hands to his chest and push him away. He was tall but not particularly muscular, so I was able to get a gap to open up between us and wrestle myself from him.

"What the hell is wrong with you?" I cried, shoving him hard.

"But I love you." He threw his hands out beseechingly. "I'm so much better for you than Freddie. I would treat you like a princess."

"How do you know how Freddie treats me? You don't."

"But he has a different girlfriend every month. Your time will be up soon, you know that."

He hit a nerve and nausea swirled in my stomach at the realisation that he was right. I had one day left before it was a month since we got together after the auction. Freddie's limit. The idea that we might be about to end something that had become so good was scary. I just had to hope that things with us were different. We got on great and I didn't think that I was needy or clingy like most of the girls he dated. The only blip had been his temper tantrum earlier and, in hindsight, maybe I overstepped. At the end of the day, he was right, he was the boss, and his decision was final.

"You have just broken so many rules, Michael," I hissed, putting my chair between us. "You shouldn't have touched me like that."

"You let Freddie touch you like that," he protested. "Is it because he's the boss?"

"No, Michael, it is not! It has nothing to do with it."

"Why not me then?"

"Because I don't think of you like that." I dragged my hands through my hair. "And you're twenty-two years of age. I'm twenty-eight. You're too young for me."

"Maybe Freddie is too old for you?" he asked, giving me a tight, expectant smile.

"He's thirty-four." Dropping my hands to my sides, I exhaled. "I won't say anything about this to anyone, but it is never to happen again. Do you hear me?"

His bottom lip jutted out and he nodded and said sulkily, "Okay. But remember when he dumps you, I'll be waiting for you."

"Okay, but I don't think I'll be taking you up on the offer." Besides, I hoped that Freddie was going to finally break his month-long time limit. "Now, just go back to your desk. Okay?"

He nodded and with his head dropped, he skulked away.

"What the hell?" I muttered as I sat back down and opened my emails. When I heard footsteps again, I sighed heavily. I couldn't do with another confrontation with Michael. When I looked up, though, my heart stopped. It wasn't Michael but Nova our receptionist. That wouldn't be so bad, but she was holding a huge bouquet of flowers. Sticking out of the top was a small white envelope with my name on it. What made me feel sick was that it was written in Freddie's handwriting.

CHAPTER SIXTEEN

"Seriously, Natty," Andrew slurred, we can't drink anymore tequila.

"Oh yes we can." My head, too heavy to keep upright, lolled forward, almost hitting the table. "I *need* to drink more tequila."

"No, what you need to do is talk to him."

He tried to put his finger on the end of my nose, but my head wouldn't stay still as his fingertip chased it. Grinning lazily, Andrew huffed out a breath and conceded defeat.

"You do need to speak to him, though, Natty."

"Nope. I don't. The flowers make it perfectly clear what he wants to say."

"You wouldn't know, though, would you? Seeing

as you threw them and the card in the bin. Why didn't you just take a peek at it?"

"What would be the point? I know what it says. Thanks for the last month but I'm not ready for a relationship. And I know that because I've had another four of them written before."

"Yours may not say that," he protested.

I waved him away with a drunken exhale and a belch. "Oops, sorry."

Andrew grimaced. "I could get drunk on your breath."

Reaching for the bowl of chips, which were now cold and soggy with vinegar, I sighed. I didn't want to think about it. I certainly didn't want to think about *Freddie* or who his next month-long relationship might be with.

"Hey, it's our song," Andrew yelled as the first few bars of the Friends theme tune sounded out. We'd adopted it as our song after we started watching it when we were about eleven. It was as we started high school and decided we needed something that was ours seeing as we were being dumped amongst a whole new group of people. We even made up a little dance. I looked at Andrew and he grinned.

"There's a little dancefloor there." I pointed

behind him. It didn't matter that there was no one else dancing. When he took a long swig of his drink, his eyes glinting over the top of his glass, I knew he was up for it.

With a little squeal we both shot out of our seat and danced our way over to the five-by-five section of tiled floor. Falling straight into our routine, we began giggling and the heaviness in my heart loosened a little bit too. For those three minutes I didn't think about Freddie. All I concentrated on was the steps that we'd created seventeen years before.

We stayed for another couple of songs, not caring that it was only us up there. The rest of the bar didn't seem to be bothered, apart from one group of girls who kept staring over and laughing. I knew what it would be. I was a bigger girl and Andrew was a good-looking guy, so why the hell was he with me. It didn't matter, though, we didn't care who was watching us. Some people were just inherently miserable and mean. Unlike me, I was full of joy. Until I thought of Freddie. As soon as he came into my head, I lost the happiness in my feet.

"I'm going to sit down," I said into Andrew's ear. "You go to the bar and order more drink."

"Are you sure?" We both swayed a little as

clearly the dancing had upset our equilibriums. Things were distinctly wobblier than they had been.

"Yep. More booze."

I wound my way back to the table and sat down with a huge sigh. I needed to think about what I was going to do after the weekend. I could face Freddie, it wouldn't be difficult, I was a big girl. Even if my heart was being squeezed dry I wouldn't show it to him. We'd agreed that we would deal with things if they didn't go well, but it didn't mean that I would find it particularly easy.

After waiting a few minutes, I pulled my phone from the pocket of my jacket and looked down at it. There was nothing from Freddie, but I shouldn't have expected there to be. He'd gone out for dinner with some prospective clients and was then taking them clubbing.

Huh, clubbing at his age. Ridiculous.

Continuing to scroll through my phone, I was distracted when Andrew arrived back with more alcohol. He cleared his throat to gain my attention.

"These are courtesy of the guy at the bar." He placed four shots on the table, and I looked over to see who our benefactor was.

"Cute." The guy was tall and blond and was wearing a suit. He appeared to be with another couple of guys who were chatting while he looked over at us. "They for me or you?"

Andrew winked. "You. He asked if he could join us. His name is Maxwell."

"If wants to he can but I'm not sure I'm in the mood. You might have to do all the talking."

I looked up at Andrew who was beckoning Maxwell over and my heart sank. I didn't want to talk to him, but he'd been nice enough to buy us drinks, I couldn't be rude. I watched as he grinned his way across to us and he made me think of another guy who wore a suit well. Not that he wore it as well as Freddie, I wasn't sure that anyone did.

"Hi, I'm Maxwell, good to meet you." He held out his hand, which I took and shook. "I believe you're Natalie."

"Yes, I am, but most people call me Natty." I pulled another stool out for him to sit. "Thanks for the drinks."

"My pleasure. Can I sit?"

Well, duh, that was why I'd pulled the stool out. God, tequila and heartache made me a bitch.

"Sure. Take a seat."

Once he was settled I instantly decided I'd made a mistake. Inviting him to come over *and* having more alcohol. The fact that the booze was there on the table though was like a personal challenge. I picked one up and knocked it back.

"Wow, you like your tequila, don't you?" Maxwell took a sip of his drink.

"I find it relaxes me."

"Relaxes her and makes her crazy," Andrew quipped, and I threw him a glare.

"I'm not crazy. I never get crazy. I'm a very dignified drunk." My chest heaved with a hiccup. "Oops, sorry."

"No problem." He had a lovely smile. All white teeth and crinkly eyes.

Andrew still hadn't sat down, so I frowned at him and nodded at his empty stool. He shook his head. "I'm just going to make a call outside."

I opened my eyes as wide as they could go, warning him. "Don't be too long," I ground out while plastering on a smile.

"I'll be back," he promised, but it didn't go unnoticed he didn't say when. I watched him leave feeling like he was walking out of my life for good. Yet, if the worse came to the worse I'd see him at home. I was being stupid.

"I thought he was your boyfriend," Maxwell said. "Until I spoke to him."

"Really?" I grabbed another shot. "How did you find out?"

"I just asked him." He moved his stool closer to mine. "He told me that you were best friends."

"We are." I grinned, mainly because I didn't know what else to say. I was not pulling out my A game with Maxwell. My heart wasn't in it. My heart was elsewhere.

"So, tell me about yourself."

I inwardly groaned. Asking me to talk about myself was lazy as far as I was concerned. A guy should ask a girl questions to find out about her.

What was I supposed to say? I'm amazing in bed, kind to children and animals and give to charity. No. It was up to him to find those things out. Maybe not the amazing in bed part, I couldn't think of him like that. Besides, we'd only just met.

That thought made me think of Freddie and how we'd had sex the first time we went out together, even if it was a work event.

"How about you find out," I replied, feeling grumpy. "Instead of me telling you."

He thought about it for a second before smiling. "Okay then, let's see how it goes."

CHAPTER SEVENTEEN

I groaned and rolled over, smacking my lips and wiping away the slobber. My head was pounding as I swallowed back the watery hint that puke was considering making an appearance. Another hangover from hell. When my hand slapped against a hard body, my heart literally stopped.

"Shit." I snatched my hand back and lay as still as a dead body. The threatened vomit rose a little higher. With panic swallowing me whole, I squeezed my eyes shut and felt down my body. "Thank god." I was fully dressed. In fact, I was still wearing my coat which was buttoned and belted. I turned my head and prayed that it was Andrew next to me. "Shit." It wasn't. It was Maxwell.

What the hell?

As stealthily as I could, I slipped off my bed, gingerly putting my feet to the floor. I didn't dare look back. I was scared that I might see a naked body on my duvet. I crept across the room and slid through the door which was already cracked open. Tiptoeing into the lounge, I almost jumped out of my skin when I saw Andrew sitting in an armchair.

"God, you scared me."

He frowned. "Why? I do live here."

"I know, but it's early. It's still dark."

Andrew burst out laughing. "No, it's not, love, you have your sunglasses on."

"I do." I gasped and my hands went to my face. "Oh, yeah. What time is it? My phone is dead."

"It's almost nine," Andrew said. "Do you want a coffee?"

I shook my head. "I think I need water."

Andrew reached down the side of the chair and when he straightened, he produced a bottle of water. "I thought you'd need it. I took it out of the freezer about an hour ago so it should be really cold."

"I love you. I want you to have my babies."

"I don't think that's likely to happen, love. I adore you but there's no way I'd put my dick near you."

"But I'm your best friend. You should be willing to do anything for me."

"And I would, just not that. It would be disgusting." He screwed up his face and shuddered. "I mean, I know I've seen your titties and your vagina and while they're very pretty, they're just not for me."

"We could use a turkey baster," I offered.

"We could but I'm not giving you your children, Natty. You'll find the love of your life for that." He started grinning and whispered, "Do you think that person might be Maxwell?"

"No. You tosser." I flopped down onto the sofa and threw him a glare. "As you can see, I'm fully dressed."

"But is he?" Andrew chuckled and hid his smile behind his mug.

I shrugged. "I don't know," I whispered, glancing over my shoulder. "I didn't dare look. I was just glad I was."

"I think maybe you should go and find out. I mean, he may well have impregnated you from outside the clothes. He looks like he might be that virile," he said with a grin.

"Did I kiss him?" I slapped a hand against my

chest over my thudding heart. "I don't think I did. I'm pretty sure I didn't. I didn't *want* to kiss him."

Andrew shook his head. "No, you didn't kiss him. He tried but you ducked it more than once."

Casting my mind back to the night before I tried to recall what Maxwell looked like. I'd been drunk when he introduced himself and continued to drink the whole time we chatted. The last thing that I could remember was him dancing with me as his two friends did shots with Andrew.

"I feel awful about it," I hissed, leaning closer to Andrew. "I can only remember that he's blond and tall, oh and that he wore a suit. I'm not one bit interested."

Andrew contemplated my words with narrow eyes. "Honest opinion?"

"Yes, honest opinion. Although, I'm not sure why it matters." Now that I was sober my heart hung heavy in my chest and there was a knot in my stomach thinking about Freddie. A grey blanket of sadness covered me, and tears pricked against my eyelashes.

"You're not interested because he's not your type. I mean, he's good looking. Not Freddie good looking, but he's good looking." He hugged his coffee mug to his chest. "But he's definitely *not* your type. Mainly, though, you're not interested because he isn't Freddie, and you were just too polite to tell him to back off."

"How did he end up here?"

Andrew looked serious as he took a breath. "The truth is I have no fucking idea. You didn't give him one bit of encouragement. In fact, you even booked him a taxi."

"Why is he even on my bed?" I whispered.

"Well, when you went to bed you left him on the sofa seeing as he missed his taxi. He must have found his way to your room in the middle of the night." Andrew's eyes went wide suddenly looking serious. "Are you sure he didn't touch you?"

I waved a hand down at myself. Still fully dressed and wearing my coat, fully buttoned and belted in exactly the way I always did it.

"I'm practically wearing a chastity belt and I might have been drunk, but I'd have known if that had happened."

"So, no dampness in your knickers then?"

"Andrew!" Sometimes he was far too inappropriate. Funny but inappropriate.

"Am I wrong?"

"No," I said with a grin. "You're not wrong. There has definitely not been any invasion down there in the last twenty-four hours." I noticed the time and thought back to waking up in Freddie's bed the day before. "Make that twenty-six hours."

Andrew met my gaze as he put his mug down. "I think it's clear that the fact he isn't Freddie is a huge factor. However, the biggest factor is that you don't actually know whether you and Freddie are over or not."

"Andrew, it's over, believe me."

He rolled his eyes. "You don't know that. Call him and ask because the bloody flowers and card have probably been dumped in the skip by the cleaners by now."

"I've sent flowers for him to enough women to know what they meant. He just happened to use a different florist." I sighed and took off my sunglasses. "I feel so sad, Andrew. I like him a lot and I thought that maybe..."

"I know, love." He moved over to kneel in front of me and took hold of my hands. "Go and get rid of lover boy in there, then we'll decide how you're going to sort the Freddie situation."

I nodded and pulled him closer to me before dropping a kiss on his forehead. Andrew stood and picked up his coffee mug on his way to the kitchen. I took a deep breath and got up to make my way back to the bedroom to get rid of Maxwell. When I was within a few steps I heard talking and so stopped, ready to creep away until he'd finished. When I heard my name, I couldn't help but hang around. Everybody liked to eavesdrop when they knew the conversation was about them, didn't they?

Then I heard, "You fucking bet me to spend the night with the big chick. It's not my fault that you didn't specify I had to shag her."

The raucous laugh that followed stuck the knife in further. While I'd heard it all before, I didn't expect to hear it in my own home and sagged against the wall. Like a masochist, I stayed there and continued to listen, my heart beating in treble time as my throat prickled with emotion.

"I couldn't even get a kiss, mate. You'd think she'd be grateful, wouldn't you... yeah, I know... fuck off, I would have earned every penny."

He went silent and I decided that I'd heard enough and marched into my room. Maxwell faced the window, his hand in his trousers' pocket, looking casual as he laughed at something being said on the other end of the line.

"Hey, dickhead," I snapped, pushing him in the back. "It's time you went."

Maxwell swung around and when he saw me,

my face must have alerted him to the fact that I'd heard every word. His pallor blanched.

"I'll call you back, Ade," he hissed down the phone.

Quick as a flash, I grabbed the phone from him. "Hey, Ade," I snapped, flashing Maxwell a sarcastic smile. "Just so you know, Maxwell didn't get a shag because his penis is far too small."

"W-what?" Ade asked as Maxwell yelled at me and tried to grab his phone.

I managed to dodge him and continued talking. "I mean I've seen a fair few penises in my time, but Maxwell's has to be the smallest, and I have a ten-month old nephew. You get what I'm saying?" *I hadn't seen his penis and I didn't have a ten-month old nephew but sometimes you had to lie to get the laugh, right?*

"Yep. I get it." Ade's voice was tight and at least he sounded contrite at being caught out.

"And for the record, *Ade,* I really hope that if you ever have a daughter, no one ever disrespects her like you and tiny dick have disrespected me." I looked Maxwell directly in the eye, including him in the conversation. "I may not have the perfect body for *you,* but it doesn't mean it's okay for you to treat me like a second-class citizen because of it. I hope you never have to know how people like *you* make people like *me* feel. I hope someone you love is never made to feel this way just because of the way they look." I then handed Maxwell his phone. "Now, get the fuck out of my home."

Turning away from Mr Tiny Dick, I walked into the kitchen where Andrew was waiting with a huge mug of coffee and a donut.

CHAPTER EIGHTEEN

When I finally charged my phone I found a message from Freddie which just said, '*I'll be round at nine.*'. He'd sent it in the early hours of Friday morning but seeing as he'd dumped me, I assumed he'd sent it by mistake.

I considered sending a message telling him, but I was struggling with staying calm and collected. If I sent a message, I would have probably come across as a scary, angry ex. I decided that I was going to simply try and act totally normal on Monday, back in the office. Be professional and calm.

As I put my hand on the door, ready to push it open, I took a deep breath. This was my moment to prove I was an adult. With that in mind and my spine straight, I breezed through the main office, saying good morning to everyone and smiling widely.

Reaching my desk, I took another fortifying breath and got myself ready to face my boss. My ex as he was now.

The door to Freddie's office was firmly closed, but the blind was open so I could see him in there through the glass panel in the wall. He was at his desk and glaring at his computer screen, not looking happy. His hair wasn't styled to perfection like normal and his tie wasn't just undone, it wasn't even there. I couldn't remember a time in the last eighteen months that I hadn't seen Freddie start the day wearing a tie.

Hesitating at my desk, I didn't know how to approach things. Did I just walk in there and ask him if he needed a coffee, like I normally did? Or did I storm in there and ask him why the hell I wasn't enough for him? When I spotted him throw his pen across the room, I decided on option three which was to stay out of his way.

I took off my coat and sat down, getting on with my daily tasks, punctuated with loud curses from next door.

When Freddie's door finally swung open, my heart began to hammer to the point I thought I might keel over. I clenched my hands into fists to hide their shaking, but my legs wouldn't stop trembling. I hated that I wanted to burst into tears just at the sight of him. If I thought too long about us being over, I knew I'd end up sobbing and possibly begging at his feet.

"Did you organise the meeting with Dominic Brown?" Freddie barked, standing in the doorway.

Shit.

"Which meeting?"

He sighed heavily and looked up to the ceiling. "The one I asked you to sort out last week. We talked about it when..." He inhaled slowly. "You were supposed to arrange for him to come in this week."

I trawled back through my memory banks and recalled a brief conversation over breakfast at his place. One of the couple of times I'd stayed over he'd talked about what we needed to think about later in the office. The conversation had never happened though. Admittedly, I'd dropped the ball on it because I should have reminded Freddie about it, and I hadn't.

"I'll contact him now. I'm sure he'll be able to fit you in." I cleared my throat and reached for the phone.

"He'd better because we need to finalise his refurb. I can't waste any more time on it." He turned to go back to his office but paused. "If he can't get here this week then I won't be happy, Natalie."

Wow. I was now Natalie. No longer Nat or even Natty.

"Sorry. It won't happen again."

"Just get it sorted."

He then disappeared but didn't close his door. That made me feel more nervous as I dialled the number and made the call. Thankfully, it wasn't a problem and triple checking Freddie's diary to avoid a mistake, the meeting was organised.

When I put the phone down I looked up to see Freddie watching me through the doorway. I would have loved to say he was gazing at me with fondness, thinking about what might have been, but he wasn't. The saying if looks could kill, certainly applied to Mr Tranter.

"I've put that in your diary," I called to him, not sure what else to say.

He nodded, pushing his chair away from his desk. I thought maybe he was just getting up to close the door between us, but he stalked over to me. When he stopped in front of my desk, arms folded, once again I wanted to cry. I'd sworn that I'd be a grown-up if things ended between us. That I wouldn't lose my cool or act all pathetic and jilted. Yet, that was exactly how I wanted to behave.

Honestly, I hadn't thought that I would feel so lost or sad. I'd truly thought it would be fun and that would be that. It was just the opposite, and I knew I couldn't work with him day after day. Not watching him with different women and having to send each of them a bouquet after their month.

"Was there something you needed?" I asked, chickening out of talking about *us*.

"Have a good night on Friday, did you?" His tone was hard and his eyes cold.

My stomach rolled at the thought of Friday and heinous Maxwell. "Not particularly. Too much tequila."

"Hmm." He nodded. "Too much tequila can be lethal. In my experience it leads to poor decisions." He leaned over at the waist, moving his hands to his trouser pockets. "Like cheating and lying. You know the sort of thing."

I frowned and sat back in my chair, more to get away from him, suffocated by his presence, unable to breath or even think. How I'd ever managed before we were having sex together I didn't know. Surely he'd always been magnetic and all encompassing. It couldn't have just been the intimate moments that had made me feel so discombobulated around him. While I stared up at him and looked into his eyes, I knew it wasn't. It was him. He was everything that I'd want for me. The sort of man I wanted to have a life with. The penis thing was a huge bonus.

"Why are you smiling?" Freddie asked.

I couldn't really say *because I thought of the word huge in the same sentence as your penis.*

"I wasn't smiling," I lied.

"Funny, I thought you were. I wondered if maybe you were smiling about whatever it was you did on Friday night." Freddie straightened. "Or whoever."

"Whoever? What are you talking about?" I pushed my chair back from the desk. He was still too close even if he wasn't in my space any longer.

"Sorry." He narrowed his eyes. "Did I say whoever? Must have been a slip of the tongue."

Freddie was being odd and if this was how he treated someone once he'd dumped them, I wasn't interested in staying around.

"I think I should give you my notice," I blurted out.

He took a half pace back and stared at me. I could see the muscle in his jaw tensing and when he took his hands from his pockets they were screwed into fists.

"New boyfriend got you a job, has he?"

"N-new boyfriend?" I frowned, not sure what he was talking ab— "Oh shit."

"Yeah," he growled. "Oh shit. I saw him leave your flat, Natalie."

I shook my head. "It was not what you think it was. I swear to you." Why the hell was I explaining myself to him? He'd dumped me. The flowers were in the skip to prove it. "Actually, I don't have to explain anything to you. Just because you don't want me it doesn't mean I should lock myself up for the rest of my life."

"What the fuck does that mean? Just because I don't want you?"

"You made it clear. On Friday." I slammed a hand on my desk, a little too hard. "Shit. That hurt."

"Are you okay?" Freddie reached out for my hand, but I refused to touch him. It would make me cry.

"I'm fine." I breathed back the tears before letting loose on what I wanted to say. "The point is, Freddie, I'm a free agent and can see who I like even if nothing happened and was never going to happen besides he was a prick who thought he could get me to sleep with him for a bet even though he had no fucking chance he wouldn't leave my flat and I woke up in my clothes including my coat and sunglasses with him on my bed when I'd left him on the sofa."

And breathe.

No comma's, no full stops and no stopping for air. I let it all out. Then I let one loan tear roll down my cheek before swiping it away.

"He fucking what?" Freddie roared.

"Which part?"

"Tell me again what he did for a bet." His fists clenched as he clearly held on tight to his anger. His face was red and the pulse in his jaw was pumping like it was a bass speaker turned up to the max.

"He bet he could get me to sleep with him. I didn't though, unless you count the fact that he came into my room in the middle of the night and—"

"*He what?*"

"I left him on the sofa, because he missed his taxi, and I was too tired and too drunk to get him another. But when I woke up he was on my bed."

"Were you alone with him?"

Freddie had turned scary. His tone was suddenly too quiet and too measured, and his hands looked like they could be murder weapons.

"Andrew was there. He tried to get him to leave,

too, but once he missed his taxi he kind of semi-passed out. We decided to just leave him there." I took a ragged breath. "He was actually okay until I found out I was a bet."

"Did you fancy him?" Dark eyes bore into me, and I shivered at their intensity.

"No. God no. He was a laugh but that was it."

"And why were you so drunk that you put yourself in danger like that?" Freddie asked, his growly tone back.

I looked at him like he was stupid, because he was. It was obvious, surely?

"I know we said if this ended, we'd be adults about it, but I wasn't. I got pissed on tequila and danced in a pub that didn't actually have a dancefloor."

Scrubbing a hand down his face, Freddie yanked the spare chair at my desk to him and sat down. He then leaned forward, resting his elbows on his thighs.

"Why would you," he said slowly, "think that we were over?"

He watched me carefully as I blinked. Was he joking?

"Well, because you dumped me." I shrugged.

"When did I dump you? What did I say to make you think I'd dumped you?"

"The flowers," I snapped. "The bloody, buggering flowers."

Freddie frowned and let out a sigh, relaxing back in the chair. "You think I sent you flowers to dump you?"

"That's what you usually do." I should know, I bloody well organised them.

"Did you read the card?" I shook my head. "The card that I actually hand wrote in the florist shop that *I* went into making me late for an important meeting. The card that came with a bouquet of flowers that *I* chose especially because they reminded me of *you*."

I thought back to the flowers. They *were* beautiful. Full blooms of wild flowers in purple, green, and white, with a fresh fragrance full of sunshine.

"They were wild flowers," I replied.

"Yeah, I know. Wild and perfect. Like you."

Wow. My heart did the swoop thing, only this time there was no feeling of nausea to go with it.

"They were?"

Freddie leaned forward again, putting a hand on my knee. "Yes. And the note was to say sorry for being a dick about the Jason Vale contract." I heard the sincerity in his voice and not for the first time in my life regretted being impetuous. "You didn't read it at all, did you?"

I shook my head. "Sorry."

"Then you went to the pub and got arseholed with Andrew and picked up some random bloke, didn't you?"

I held up my finger. "Kind of, but in my defence I didn't fancy him and had no intention of doing anything with him. And I didn't pick him up, he came over to me."

"But you still let him sleep on your sofa?" I nodded again. "And you didn't think to call me to talk about what you thought had happened." I shook my head. "And you didn't wonder what I meant when I texted you to say I'd be at yours for nine the following morning?" I shook my head.

"I didn't see it until later because my phone lost charge, and I was too hungover to check it."

Freddie breathed out slowly. "So, all weekend, we've both been miserable thinking the other one has dumped them?" I nodded, but this time with a small smile and an extra little buzz in my veins. "When we could have been shagging all *bloody weekend*, seeing as I had cleared it so I could spend it just with you, without interruption or distraction?"

"You did?" I said on a breathy sigh.

"I did, you idiot." He rolled his eyes. "What happened to the flowers? Which cost me a fortune by the way."

I grimaced. "I put them and the card in the bin. I did think they were a little larger than your usual break up flowers."

"Too bloody right. Forty quid max for a break up!"

"Except for Josie," I said, cringing. "I paid more for hers because I liked her."

Freddie burst out laughing. "God, no wonder I love you."

That was when I fell off my chair.

CHAPTER NINETEEN

"Are you okay?" Freddie asked. Grinning he held out his hand to help me up off the floor. "Was it something I said?"

I let him pull me up while I tried to regulate my breathing. I knew that I'd heard him right but wasn't sure why he'd said it? We were getting on well, the sex was beyond amazing, and apart from a communication issue re dumping, we worked well together. My heart was absolutely aware that I was falling in love with him – okay, *had* fallen in love with him. The surprise, though, was that Freddie felt the same way.

Settling back on my chair, I gripped the seat and stared at him to see he was still grinning.

"W-what did you say, exactly?"

"I said that I love you." He sat back in the chair, shoving his hands into his trouser pockets. That casual way he always did, looking so bloody relaxed. Like it didn't matter that he'd just broken the biggest piece of news ever.

"Love." I repeated.

"Yes, gorgeous, love." He stretched his legs out and crossed them at the ankles. "Any problem with that?"

"Nope," I croaked.

"I don't expect you to reply, if that's what you're worried about." One hand came from his trouser pocket to push his hair back from his face. Nonchalance personified. "After all, I'm about nine months ahead of you in this." He waved a finger between us.

"Yeah, I know that but..." I blew out my cheeks.

"Don't think about it. Let's just go with the flow and maybe try talking to each other rather than getting drunk or sulking all weekend."

"You sulked?" I asked.

Freddie arched a brow. "Yeah, big time. My mum sent me home from Sunday lunch because she said I was being a baby. In fact, she told me that no wonder you'd gone and got yourself a new fella if I behaved like that."

I gasped. "What did you do? And you told your family about me?"

"I gave my brother a dead arm and called my sister a shit head. And yes, I've been telling them about you for months. When we finally got together I announced it at Sunday lunch."

"You told your family over Yorkshire pudding and sprouts that we were having sex?"

"God no," he replied looking shocked. "None of us eat sprouts. Vile things."

I laughed quietly and watched as Freddie's beautiful smile spread across his face, crinkling his eyes at the corners.

"I told them that we were together," he continued. "That I really liked you and that I hoped it would go somewhere."

"When was that?" I asked, tentative because I had a feeling the answer might floor me.

"The Sunday after the auction."

That was just two days after we first had sex. He'd told his family that he hoped our thing would go somewhere, just forty-eight hours after he'd given me the first experience of his orgasm giving skills.

Leaning forward and removing his hands from his pockets, he grabbed the seat of my chair and wheeled it closer to him. Opening his legs so that me and my chair nestled between them, he held my face between his hands, and touched his forehead to mine. I felt like the most treasured possession anyone had ever had. The safety and love that he passed through his touch was like nothing I'd ever had in a relationship before. Other than my parents who had to love me like that, it was their job after all. Freddie, though, made me feel like I could do or be anything. Like I was the most beautiful woman on earth, and he knew how lucky he was to have me. That feeling was entirely mutual.

"I love you too," I whispered, my lips brushing against Freddie's.

"I know," he replied.

"Confident much?"

He shrugged. "I'm a very self-assured and poised kind of guy."

I giggled and sagged into his arms as he wrapped them around me, overwhelmed with the relief that we were okay.

"What exactly did you write on the card for the flowers?" I asked.

"It was almost poetry. How sorry I was and what a bloody idiot I'd been and that I'd make it up to you with my enormous penis."

"That was the poetry bit, I take it?" I rubbed my cheek against his stubble and sighed.

"Yeah, I think rhyming heinous with penis was genius."

I laughed softly, content in being wrapped in his arms. "I'm sorry I threw it and the flowers away. I was stupid."

"It's fine, gorgeous," he said, tucking a strand of hair behind my ear. "I'll buy you some more."

"You will?"

"Yeah, but one thing they won't ever be is break-up flowers."

When he kissed me softly, I knew he was telling the truth.

CHAPTER TWENTY

FREDDIE

To say that I was nervous was an understatement. I was shitting my pants. What I was about to do was even scarier than the day I'd taken my driving test. Believe me, that was fucking scary, especially when I got Big Mary as my examiner. She was known for either failing you or flirting with you. Lucky for me, I knew how to charm the ladies *and* drive a car.

Anyway, apart from that experience, this was the one that had my stomach gurgling with nerves.

"You look like you're about to piss yourself," Jacob said, his laughing face on my phone screen.

I'd video messaged him to get a bit of moral support and had shared some air time with his cute five-month-old, Theo. Rebecca had then taken him for his nap, leaving me with the less cute Jacob.

"It's a big thing that I'm about to do. It's the rest of my life."

"Yeah, and you're sure about it, aren't you?"

"Too fucking right."

"Well, stop worrying then." He gave a deep chuckle. "I don't think I've ever seen you so rattled."

I scrubbed a hand down my face. "I've got half an hour to sort myself out. What do I do?"

"Grab a stiff drink," he replied, "and look at a picture of Natty to remind yourself why you're putting yourself through it."

It wasn't a bad idea, and I knew which picture I could look at. It was one of her in her lacy red underwear and high red shoes. She was looking over her shoulder at me as I caught her getting dressed. There was the most sublime smile on her face and her eyes were shining with love for me. That photo was also the reason why we were late for dinner with her mum and dad. If I recalled, and I did very well, she wore those red shoes while I made her scream with my tongue followed by my dick. Let's say she was more than satisfied by the time we left for the restaurant.

"Okay," I said, straightening my shoulders. "I'm ready. Let's do this."

"Good man." Jacob high-fived the screen.

"Ugh, you cheesy bastard. Don't ever do that again, okay?"

He winked at me and offered another high five before I ended the call.

When Nat let herself in I thought I was going to puke. This was it. This was when I hopefully set my life on the path that it was meant to be on.

"Oh my god," Nat cried as she flopped down onto the sofa. "You should have seen what Rose was wearing today at work." She frowned. "Where were you anyway? There weren't any meetings in your diary."

I sneaked off after the monthly meeting, just shouting that I'd see her here later. It was because I couldn't look at her without thinking I might give the game away. Plus, I had some cooking to do, and it was not something that came naturally to me. I tended to survive on pre-packed salads and soup before Nat.

Actually, everything before Nat was pretty crap if I was honest.

"What's that smell?" She sat up straight and sniffed the air. "Have you been cooking because that actually smells good."

Grinning proudly, I nodded. "I made sweet and sour chicken with rice."

"Oh Freddie," she sighed. "That's my favourite."

"I know." I grinned, feeling proud. "It's taken me hours, but I did it all by myself. From scratch. Even the sauce." I didn't tell her that batch ended up in the bin, with the saucepan, and I'd had to go out and buy a jar.

Standing and wrapping her arms around my waist, she cuddled into me, and a wave of love swept over me. Love and confidence in what I was going to do. While my heart filled my chest to capacity, it suddenly hit me that I didn't need the fancy limo which would be on its way in a couple of hours. The empty ballroom which I'd hired out, the one the auction had been held in, wasn't necessary, nor the three-piece band who were going play while I asked her the most important question of my life. Not even the penthouse suite in the best hotel in the city was required. All I needed to do it was me and her. Me and *my* woman. Me and *my* Nat.

"Nat," I whispered, slipping my hand into my trouser pocket.

"Hmm." She tightened her hold on me. "What, baby?"

I took a deep breath. "Will you marry me?"

She stilled and for a moment my heart stopped. For an instant I thought she might say no but then she pulled her head back and looked up at me. Her beautiful eyes shone with unshed tears and there was the biggest smile on those gorgeous, plump lips of hers.

"Really?"

I chuckled. "Yes, really. I would love you to marry me, gorgeous. I want to spend the rest of my life with you." I held out the small black box that I'd taken from my pocket. "I hope you like it. I can change it if you don't."

Slowly lifting the lid, I watched Nat to see her reaction. I would know instantly if she didn't like it. When her eyes landed on the pear-shaped diamond on a platinum band, she gasped and slapped a hand over her mouth while the other tentatively reached out to touch it.

"Oh my goodness," she said quietly. "It's beautiful, Freddie. Can I put it on?"

"Well that depends." I shrugged. "Whether you say yes or not."

"Yes! Yes, of course it's yes."

Smiling, I took the ring out and threw the box in the general direction of the sofa. Nat held out her hand, wiggling her fingers, and as soon as I pushed it on she squealed and jumped up and down on the spot.

"You don't want to change it?"

"No way. Don't you dare." Her gaze never left the diamond which twinkled in the light of the candles and lamps around the room. She looked at it like it might be about to do something magical. Finally, she looked up at me. "I love you so much. Thank you for asking me to be your wife."

"From the minute I kissed you, there's never been any doubt about it. It was only ever going to be you. You're my one. The person who makes every day worthwhile. You are my beating heart."

"Oh wow," she said with a gasp. "You're so good."

I grinned and gave her a cheesy wink. "You know what else I'm good at?"

She didn't need to think about it but took my hand and led me out of the lounge. When we got to the door, she stopped and gasped.

"What?" I asked.

"Can I make a request?"

I ran a finger down her cheek, marvelling at how beautiful she was. "What's that, gorgeous?"

"Can we go sheep shearing in Wales on our honeymoon?"

"God, I love you. Is there any chance we can have a shag now?" I asked.

She nodded enthusiastically and went back to dragging me to the bedroom.

Let's just say that sweet and sour chicken with rice is great for breakfast.

The End

P.S. They did go sheep shearing and bought a stuffed toy lamb, Donut, which was loved dearly by their baby daughter, Coco, who was born a year later.

ABOUT THE AUTHOR

Nikki lives in Cheshire with her husband, two dogs, and lovely mother-in-law who supplies her with endless cups of tea. She writes romance with a touch of humour and lots of love, and hopes that she puts a smile on her reader's faces and a sigh in their heart.

Her ambitions of becoming a writer started at the age of 10 when she started writing poetry at school, and was given the honour of reading one of her poems to the rest of her year group (a truly embarrassing experience that she will never forget).

Nikki is grateful for the wide variety of strange and wonderful people in her life, otherwise, she'd never know what to write about! She always takes a keen interest in family and friends, finding out their innermost secrets in readiness for her next book.

For updates on future releases check out her social media links.

facebook.com/NikkiAshtonBooks

twitter.com/NikkerAsh

instagram.com/nikkiashtonauthor

ALSO BY NIKKI ASHTON

Standalones

(All books are standalone stories, with 'guest' appearances from characters in the previous book)

Guess Who I Pulled Last Night?

No Bra Required

Get Your Kit Off

Cheese Tarts & Fluffy Socks

Roman's Having Sex Again

The Big Ohhh!

Do You Do Extras?

Pelvic Flaws

Snake Bandit (YA)

*

Connor Ranch Stories

(Contemporary Romance)

Box of Hearts (Single Dad, Second Chance)

Angels' Kisses (Second Chance)

Secret Wishes (YA)

*

Cooper Brothers

(Contemporary, Second Chance Romance)

Elijah

Samuel

*

Love in Dayton Valley

(Standalone Romantic Humour)

The Triple Threat (Friends-to-Lovers)

The Jackpot Screwer (Surprise Baby)

The Beef Game (Single Dad, Second Chance)

The Bitch List (Enemies-to-Lovers)

*

Maddison High School

(Contemporary, British High School, Enemies-to-Lovers Romance)

Hate Struck

Love Struck

*

Rock Stars Don't Like

(Standalone Romantic Humour)

Rock Stars Don't Like Big Knickers (Single Mum)

Rock Stars Don't Like Ugly Bras (Enemies-to-Lovers)

Rock Stars Do Like Christmas Stockings (Secret Romance)

Rock Stars Don't Like Sparkly Thongs

*

The Warrior Creek Series

(Standalone Rock Star Romance)

The Last Chorus (*Friends-to-Lovers*)

The Opening Line - Coming 2023

The First Chord - Coming 2024

The Final Beat - Coming 2025

Printed in July 2023
by Rotomail Italia S.p.A., Vignate (MI) - Italy